MW01115149

Misery Range
Bay of Bountiful
Eden Glade
Mt Molar
Twisty River
Grandad's Gully
Cascade Canyon
Puzzling Plains
Col
Cliffs of Calamity
Mt Monstrous
Mother's Knee Hill
Ridge of Rising Flame
Swamp of Children's Wishes
Tree of Wailing Witches
Meadow of Dreams
Ancient Forest
Mystic
Home
Lunch Pass
The ISLAND
Home Lagoon
Granny's Pass
Paradise Peninsula

Basin
Three Sisters
Bow Beach
N
W
E
S
Pancake Rocks
Forest
Fox Glacier
Fearsome Fjords
Mt Difficulty
Dragon's Crater
Putrid Plains
Clappers' Saddle
Eastern Bays
tains
Mt Astonishing
Gulp Swallow Pass
Boiling Stream
Magic Terraces
Fairy Falls
Lake Levitation
zor Reef

For aunties Fiona, Rachel,
Niamh, and Sarah
-JR

Published by Dragon Brothers Books Ltd
www.dragonbrothersbooks.com
© 2017 James Russell. Illustrations © 2017 Dragon Brothers Books.
A catalogue record for this book is available from the National Library of New Zealand. The
moral rights of the author have been asserted. This book is copyright. Except for the purposes
of fair reviewing no part of this publication may be reproduced or transmitted in any form or
by any means, electronic or mechanical, including photocopying or recording, or stored in any
information storage and retrieval system, without permission in writing from the publisher.
ISBN: 978-0-473-43530-1
Digital animations created by Courtney White
Cover illustration: Kerem Beyit
Internal vignettes: Suleyman Temiz
Chapter icon: istock
Editing: Sue Copsey

THE ༄ DRAGON DEFENDERS

BOOK THREE

An Unfamiliar Place

A Dragon Brothers Book by

JAMES RUSSELL

"I would have kept reading it all night if I was allowed!"

Zach Norwood, age 9

"Best book I've ever read!"

Alison Lee-Joe, age 10

"So daring and adventurous! Briar is so sneaky and courageous!"

Charlotte Pervan, age 9

"It formed a movie in my mind!"

George Smith, age 10

"One of my top five favourite books ever!"

Sam McKissock, age 9

www.dragonbrothersbooks.com

Sign up to find out when the next chapter book in the series comes out.

Simply visit **www.dragonbrothersbooks.com** and enter your email address. We'll keep you updated on new books, and we'll send you an email whenever anything cool happens!

Books in the series

Or, for younger readers

The Dragon Brothers Trilogy

The Dragon Defenders series grew out of The Dragon Brothers Trilogy
– children's picture books for children aged 3-7.

How to use this book

This book is unlike any other you've seen. Of course, it works just like a normal book; you start reading at the start, and read right through to the end. That will work just fine.

But you can also enjoy it another way. You can download the free 'AR Reads' app onto a smartphone or tablet, point it at parts of the book and watch it become reality.

Your choice!

Here's how:

Step 1. Download the free 'AR Reads' app*.
You'll find this on the App Store, or on Google Play.

Step 2. Start up the app.

Step 3. Follow the set-up instructions.

Step 4. Point your device's camera at the pictures on the pages marked with a phone/tablet at the bottom.

*If you already have the AR Reads app downloaded onto your device, you'll need to check for updates in order for the app to work on The Dragon Defenders – Book Three.
To use this app, your device will need to have an internet connection.

CHAPTER 1

Briar did exactly as she was told. She knew it would have been foolish not to.

She sat down before the computer screen, not daring to look at her uncle – The Pitbull – who stood behind her, gripping the back of her chair. He was furious. He positively vibrated with rage. She could hear him grinding his teeth.

"Press play," growled The Pitbull. He sounded more like a wild animal than a human.

Briar clicked on the mouse, and the video began to play. It took her a moment to work out exactly what

she was seeing, but as soon as she did, she knew
she was in deep trouble. Her heart sank.

The scene was of the deck of a ship. The Pitbull's
ship. The date in the top corner of the screen
showed that the video was taken three weeks ago.
It was night.

As the camera panned back and forth, Briar could
see The Pitbull's black helicopter, looking like a giant
insect in the darkness, crouched and ready to spring

into the air. It trembled, buffeted by a terrific wind. A flag flapped furiously on a pole. The deck of the ship was slick and shiny with sea water – showered every few seconds by great plumes of spray. Waves crashed against the side of the ship, rising up and over it, driven before the wind.

The camera turned again. Four cages could be seen quite clearly in the glare of the ship's floodlights. Briar could also see the magnificent dragons housed in three of them.

Then, something in the video caught Briar's eye. A boy appeared. Flynn. She knew his name from hearing her uncle and his men talk endlessly about him and his brother Paddy – the two boys from the island where the dragons live. He was marched at gunpoint by The Pitbull's men. He looked defiant – unbeaten and brave.

Then The Pitbull came on screen, stalking across the deck towards the boy. It sent a chill down Briar's spine.

Suddenly, she saw herself. From the point of view of the men and her uncle, she would have been almost impossible to spot – hidden by the dragons' cages. But, from this angle – the security camera must have been mounted high on a pole – she was in plain sight. She moved quickly around the cages, gently easing back the bolts to the heavy steel doors.

Suddenly, a huge green dragon, with a small boy clinging to its back, swooped in front of the camera like a giant eagle. The boy, of course, was Paddy. Beneath his dragon swung a huge net, bulging with something heavy. Briar knew it contained nine of The Pitbull's men, captured by the brave boy. The dragon released its grip, dropping the net onto the deck. The men tumbled out; battered, bruised, and frightened out of their wits. It caused The Pitbull to reel backwards in shock. Before any of the men could recover, Flynn bolted, sprinting for the railing and leaping over it. But he caught his foot on the top, and went tumbling end over end into the darkness below. The Pitbull fired his gun, but Flynn had gone.

Briar watched herself racing frantically around the cages, taking advantage of the confusion on deck. She swung all the doors open, then stood well back. The dragons didn't move. They simply sat in their cages and gazed towards the open doors. They couldn't understand that they were free. In the short time they had been imprisoned, their wild spirits had been sorely damaged.

Briar remembered the terrible fear that had coursed through her body when she made up her mind to do what she did next. She'd hesitated, uncertain and afraid. Then, a kind of reckless excitement had struck her, and she'd dashed into the cage that held the cobalt blue dragon with the shimmering gold wings.

On the video she watched herself coming alongside the dragon's head, grabbing one of its spines and pulling it, desperately, towards the open cage door. She looked so tiny beside the colossal creature. But the dragon remained where it was, staring straight ahead. It was as if Briar wasn't even there.

She stopped pulling and let go. Standing directly in front of the dragon, she looked into its eyes. Briar remembered pleading with it to move. Then, she put out her hand and rested it gently on the dragon's nose.

The dragon lifted its head and seemed to see Briar for the first time. It shook itself, like a dog – a shudder that began at its head and ran down its enormous body to its tail. Slowly, the huge animal rose to its feet. Briar backed away, keeping her eyes locked with the dragon's, her hand raised in front of her. It followed her, stepping slowly, deliberately, as if in a trance. As it emerged from its cage, its giant wings unfolded like a pop-up children's book. The dragon flapped them once, twice. It turned its huge head towards the other two dragons, and although there was no sound on the video, Briar remembered the noise it had made – a series of short, sharp barks. It roused the other dragons, who rose and clambered out from their own cages.

Briar kept desperately looking across to the men, many of whom were staring over the railing into the wild sea, trying to spot Flynn through the flying spray. Others looked up into the sky, searching for the green dragon, afraid it might return. The Pitbull stood in the centre of the deck, gazing dumbly upwards into the dark.

None of them thought to check the cages.

In seconds, all three dragons had escaped, springing aloft and flapping furiously against the wind. Then Briar, too, was gone, slipping quickly back into the shadows like a thief in the night.

Suddenly there came a blaze of light, and every man on deck looked up. One of the dragons had sent a river of fire across the night sky. Some, including The Pitbull, cowered in terror. Briar could see the twinkling flashes of the men's guns as they shot aimlessly into the darkness.

When the shooting finally ceased, The Pitbull turned towards the cages and his jaw dropped open. Briar saw his silent scream of anger as he dropped to his knees. His men ran to the cages and examined the locks, shaking their heads in disbelief. Some of them went inside the cages, as if checking to see whether the dragons hadn't simply been lost in a dark corner. Briar couldn't help but giggle.

The video came to an end and the screen went dead. There was no sound, save for the soft whirr of the computer's cooling fan. Briar remained seated, staring straight ahead.

Then, she felt the frightening weight of her uncle's hand gripping her shoulder. At the same time, he barked out an order.

"Lock her up."

CHAPTER 2

Everything looked different upside down. But by now, Flynn was almost used to it. Whenever he squeezed his knees together, and pulled back sharply on Iris's spines – the command for the dragon to pull up – she did the complete opposite. Instead, she flipped over onto her back and dived vertically for the ground.

The first time it happened, Flynn almost fell. He screamed out in horror and made a flailing grasp for the dragon – any part of her. He just managed to grab around her neck, while his legs swung freely over five hundred feet of thin air. It was terrifying.

Above him, Iris made a snickering sound. Flynn had come to understand that it was the dragon's way of laughing, or at least of letting him know she was enjoying herself hugely. Thankfully, Flynn had discovered a way of staying on Iris's back even when she was upside down – he moved his feet backwards and hooked his heels under the leading edge of her wing. The trick was to do it quickly, before she flipped.

"Iris!" he yelled, pulling hard on one spine. Obediently, and as quick as lightning, she flipped over again, levelling off at high speed. "Naughty dragon!" he scolded, but she only snickered again and Flynn couldn't help but smile.

Aside from the flying upside down trick, Flynn and Iris had come to understand each other, and now flew together with great skill. They'd come a long way from that first flight, Flynn realised. That day he'd clung on for dear life while Iris bravely battled both The Pitbull's helicopter and the effects of a tranquilliser dart fired into her body by one of the pilots. It was always going to be a losing battle, and Flynn only vaguely remembered the crash-landing in the forest and the terrible force with which his head had struck a log.

Flynn urged Iris into a steady climb and marvelled afresh at the immense strength of her huge golden wings as she powered up into the clear blue sky. At well over two thousand feet, they levelled off again and Flynn let her glide while they took in the view. He could see every corner of the island from here. It was awash with colour, from the sparkling-white snow-capped peaks of Mt Astonishing and Mt Monstrous, to the dense, dark green of the Colossal Forest, spread like an enormous blanket across the land. Fringing the island was the turquoise blue of the reef, and further out, the deeper blue of the ocean depths. They were separated by a dazzling line of foaming white surf.

Down there, everything hummed and moved. Forests teemed with birds, mammals and insects. Around the ocean reefs fish, crustaceans, dolphins and whales were all busy going about their business. But up here, it was different – a silent, still, awe-inspiring dragon's-eye view. It gave Flynn a new appreciation of the beauty of their paradise island home.

From high above, Flynn heard a faint shout – Paddy! Moments later, a slash of emerald green and orange streaked past them towards the earth. Flynn felt the blast of wind. Their pet dragon, Elton, and his brother were diving so fast they were just a blur, and in only a few seconds were no more than a speck, far below. Flynn heard a piercing "*Squee!*" and Lightning, their pet falcon, whizzed past him too, plummeting towards the ground. The bird was travelling at the speed of an arrow, faster even than Elton.

Flynn didn't hesitate. He lunged sideways and forwards, and Iris responded so fast it took his breath away. They sped after Lightning, Elton, and Paddy, descending so quickly that Flynn had the alarming feeling the land was rushing up to meet them.

Paddy and Elton had levelled out and turned north, still rocketing along, powered by the momentum of the dragon's dive. Elton's giant wings, coloured with all the orange hues of a sunset, were raked backwards – as streamlined as he could possibly make them. Iris struggled to keep up. She couldn't quite match Elton for speed, but being slightly smaller, she could turn more quickly.

Paddy guided Elton to the northernmost part of the Colossal Forest, then turned west, following the path of the Twisty River. Flynn saw where they were heading, and cut the corner. Soon, they were no more than a hundred yards behind. Flynn laughed as he watched Paddy guide Elton so low that his talons dragged in the river, throwing up a rooster tail of spray.

As they flew, the banks of the Twisty River rose on either side and the river looped back and forth. They had entered Grandad's Gully – so named because their grandfather had once fallen down the steep bank into the rushing river, while on a fishing trip. The powerful current had swept him downstream, deep into the Cascade Canyon. Eventually he'd made it to the river's edge, dragging himself onto a tiny shingle beach. But he could go neither upstream nor down and was quite imprisoned by the canyon's high rock walls. He certainly didn't fancy getting back into the river.

There was firewood on the stony beach, and flint rock all around. He'd survived on the fish he could catch – somehow, through the entire ordeal, he'd managed to hold onto his fishing rod!

It was one of the boys' favourite stories. They particularly loved the part when their grandmother finally found him. She'd searched night and day, and was exhausted and sick with worry. But when she came to the top of the cliff and peered over, to her surprise her husband appeared to be having a wonderful time! He was singing at the top of his voice, while swimming naked in the river!

He cavorted and splashed about like a little child.

Back on the beach, skewered on branches, two fat

fish sizzled above a merry little fire.

Astonished, she'd called down to him. He hadn't

seemed in the least bit surprised. In fact, he'd called

back, "My dear, you're just in time for dinner!" The boys

always fell about laughing at that part of the story.

As they passed over that very beach, Iris closed

the gap even more, until they were almost on

Elton's tail.

Paddy turned around and grinned widely

at Flynn. "Race you to the sea!" he yelled, urging

Elton to fly even faster.

Iris knew this game, and snickered loudly before

letting forth a bellowing roar – a challenge to Elton.

Elton roared back, furiously flapping his wings

before they reached the trickiest part of the Cascade

Canyon, where it would be too narrow to do so.

Lightning, who seemed to magically disappear and

then reappear without warning, was suddenly with them again, flying alongside the dragons and deftly avoiding their powerful wings.

The canyon walls widened and then narrowed as they tore above the tumbling rapids of the river. The two dragons banked through the tight bends so quickly that Flynn felt light-headed. The boys could do little now but hold on tight. When their dragons flew like this, they ignored the brothers' commands, flying on pure instinct. They loved nothing more than to fly at the very edge of their ability, despite how terrifying it was for their riders.

Banking around a narrow bend in the canyon, Iris saw her chance. The cliffs either side widened slightly where the river straightened out and there was just enough room for a few powerful flaps of her wings. Being smaller, she could accelerate faster than Elton. Flynn gave a shout of panic as she surged, coming up alongside Elton. He saw his brother look nervously across at them. At the end of the short straight, through perhaps the narrowest part of the canyon, he spotted the blue stripe of the sea; the finish line! But there was room for only one dragon, as far as Flynn could see. Lightning squawked in alarm, pulling up and out, wisely opting to view the rest of the competition from above. Elton and Iris, however, had other ideas. Neck and neck, they hurtled towards the gap at frightening speed. One thing was clear: if they struck even a glancing blow off the side of the canyon they could all be killed.

As the two dragons reached the gap, they performed an incredible feat. In perfect unison, both flipped on their side, one wingtip almost touching the river, the other pointing to the sky. Now, the dragons were back-to-back, which brought Flynn and Paddy so close together they almost knocked heads.

"Watch out!" yelled Paddy. He clung to Elton, making himself as flat against the dragon as he could. Flynn did the same. The dragons came even closer together. Parts of their wings actually touched.

In this way, the two dragons sped through the gap in the canyon with just inches to spare! Flynn even heard the clack of Iris's talons striking the rock wall as she passed through the narrowest point.

As soon as they were through, the dragons levelled and both let out great roars and bright streams of fire. Emerging from the shade of the Cascade Canyon out into the glittering brightness over the open sea, Paddy and Flynn couldn't help themselves either; they whooped with joy and laughed with relief.

"We won!" Paddy yelled to Flynn, grinning broadly.

"Sure you did," laughed Flynn. "Second place."

"*Squee!*" Lightning was back, swooping skilfully down and neatly landing on Iris's head. He loved nothing more than to hitch a ride on the dragons. Iris responded with a playful bark of greeting to the bird. Not for the first time, Flynn wondered at the close connection that seemed to exist between the falcon and the two dragons. He'd read somewhere that dinosaurs and birds were closely related. How well did birds and dragons understand each other?

Flynn guided Iris out to the edge of the reef for one of their favourite games – riding the updraft created by an incoming swell. Paddy and Elton followed close behind. Today the waves were huge and groomed perfectly smooth by a gentle offshore breeze. Flynn and Iris glided out to where they rose from the deep, pushed upwards by the reef. Iris didn't have to flap her wings at all, she simply positioned herself in front of the wave where the air rose up the face before it. It was a trick they had copied from the flocks of gannets patrolling for fish, and Iris loved it. She tore along the face of the wave until the very last second before the wave finally reared up and broke, then rose and banked hard, turning back out to sea to catch another one.

In this manner they flew south, along the coast towards the brothers' house and Home Lagoon. Lightning's incredible eyes spied something tasty to eat on the shoreline and he raced away in pursuit.

Finally, they rounded the small headland just west of the lagoon, and the boys eagerly scanned the bay. Last night there had been a full moon, which meant their grandparents were due today. In fact, they should have arrived by now. But there was no sign of their yacht anchored in the harbour.

Flynn looked across at Paddy, who shrugged his shoulders.

As they drew closer, Paddy caught sight of Ada, their little sister, running out of the house and onto the beach to greet them. She waved and skipped back and forth as the two dragons glided in and landed.

The boys slipped off their backs. Iris made gentle snickering sounds of greeting and Elton immediately lay down so that Ada could crawl onto his back. He was terribly fond of her. She giggled and playfully pulled his spines and tickled his neck. Elton released a puff of smoke which made her cough. The brothers laughed.

Flynn and Paddy were buzzing after their ride, but saddle-sore from flying for so long. They were also hungry.

It was perfect timing; their father came out of the house and called them all in for dinner. Flynn gathered Ada up in his arms and the brothers ran up the steps onto the verandah of their home to greet him. But, before they went inside, the boys and their father turned back to look out across the ocean. All three scanned the horizon, searching the endless blue for the tiny white sail of their grandparents' yacht.

"Strange," said their father.

"Have they ever been late before?" asked Paddy.

"No," he replied. "But they're sailing into a head wind, so perhaps that's slowed them down. Go on inside. Let's eat."

The boys tumbled into the house and kissed their mother, both talking at once, excited to tell her about their day. Their father, however, remained on the verandah for a moment more, his forehead creased with worry.

CHAPTER 3

After sending Briar away to be locked up, The Pitbull felt much better. He had one of his men run him a freezing bath into which he lowered himself. The cold water helped him to think, and was supposed to be good for the skin.

As he lay in the bath and gazed out over the city through the floor-to-ceiling windows, he allowed himself some small congratulations. Everything was coming together nicely. It was like a game of chess – he would simply win the game, one move at a time.

Yet he couldn't help feeling a flush of anger as he thought about the past ten months. There was no getting around it – he had failed to capture a dragon from the brothers' horrible island not once, but twice.

The first time, it had been the brothers themselves who had somehow captured his men and spoiled his plans to obtain a dead dragon and a live dragon's egg. The fools he'd sent to carry out the mission had brought home nothing more than an egg-shaped rock. For nine months he'd cared for that rock, waiting for it to hatch, until finally he could bear it no longer. He'd taken to it with a jackhammer and split it in two, revealing nothing but solid grey stone. The very thought of it brought on a furious twitching of his eye – an uncontrollable tic that seemed to happen whenever he lost his temper these days.

The second time, he'd taken matters into his own hands. He'd purchased a ship and two helicopters and recruited a small army of well-trained men.

But once again, all of his plans had come to nothing. However, this time he'd failed not only because of the brothers' meddling, but also that of his own family. Briar – his red-headed devil of a niece – had freed the three dragons on the ship without a thought for his feelings!

To rub salt into the wound, the boy – Flynn – had destroyed the remaining helicopter, as well as the ship's engines. For ten days they'd floated adrift on the open sea, helplessly blown about before the wind. Somehow the anchor had been lost. He himself had tossed the last radio unit overboard in a fit of rage, so they couldn't even call for rescue. Luckily, they'd eventually been spotted by a passing freighter ship, and a tugboat had been dispatched to tow them back to the mainland.

Shamed and disgusted, The Pitbull had returned home to lick his wounds. For three days, he'd done little but stare out of the window, thinking about the best way to have his revenge. He didn't eat or sleep. He didn't wash or shave. His eyes turned red, bloodshot from lack of sleep. His accountants and managers had all come to see him, begging him to turn his attention to his many businesses and criminal operations. He'd sent them all away.

He was obsessed. He could think only of catching the brothers, and what he would do with them when he did.

Then, he'd had a brainwave. He ordered his men to build a new prison in preparation for the brothers' capture. He had two cells built, side by side, on the thirty-ninth floor of his high-rise tower. It was of the very highest security – completely impossible to break out of. Even if they somehow managed to escape the cells, there was no way they could get to the ground floor. A security code was needed to get into the lift, and another one to operate it. Half a dozen security cameras had been installed. It was, of course, far too high for the boys to jump out of a window without killing themselves. He'd made sure the windows were too small to escape out of anyway. He'd worked out every detail. He'd even planned what food they'd be served – nothing but horse and falcon meat.

It was only when the prison was completed that The Pitbull realised he didn't have a clue about how to catch the brothers. By this point, he was demented. He hadn't slept for nearly a week. His eyes were frightening to look at. He was weak from not eating. He couldn't take it any more. He called for the doctor, who gave him some powerful sleeping pills. He drank a large glass of whiskey, and then another. Finally, mercifully, he'd fallen asleep.

When The Pitbull awoke twenty hours later, he'd felt much better – apart from a slight headache. He'd lain in bed, thinking about his next move. Of one thing he was sure: the brothers couldn't be caught on their island. They knew it too well, and they were too fast and clever to simply be trapped.

Suddenly, he'd sat bolt upright in his bed and smacked his forehead hard with the flat of his hand. Of course! Why hadn't it occurred to him before? If he couldn't catch the boys, they would just have to come to him. And he knew exactly how to do it. It was so simple he couldn't help but laugh. It was the perfect plan. It was nothing short of brilliant.

And once the brothers were safely out of the way, he could catch as many dragons from the island as he pleased!

The Pitbull had leapt out of bed that morning, shouting for his men. He'd ordered an enormous breakfast, over which he briefed them all on what to do. They'd left excitedly, as anxious as he was to have their revenge on the brothers. The Pitbull finished his breakfast and went to his office, his energy renewed.

Within four hours his men had returned.

"Your orders have been carried out," said one of them.

"Did they put up a fight?" enquired The Pitbull.

"Not really. It was almost too easy."

"Don't get cocky," said the Pitbull.

"No sir."

"Was there a ring?" asked The Pitbull.

"Yes sir." The man placed it on the desk. It was silver, with a single emerald.

"Good. Lock them in the tower – in the new cells."

His men hurried away.

At that moment, one of The Pitbull's technical staff had entered his office. He'd stood before his boss's desk, nervously wringing his hands.

"What?" said The Pitbull, not looking up.

"Sir. I think there's something you should see, sir," said the man.

"Well, what is it? I don't have time for your brainless muttering. Spit it out, you idiot!"

"Well, sir. It's… it's something you might find upsetting…"

"If you don't tell me what it is right now, you'll be the one who finds it upsetting – when I feed you to the lion!"

"Yes, sir. Sorry, sir. It's… it's your niece, sir – Briar. We've just watched the video footage taken from the ship, sir. She was the one who freed the dragons."

But now he'd taken care of that little problem, too. Briar could live out the rest of her life in her jail cell for all he cared. Taking a deep breath, The Pitbull plunged under the water.

CHAPTER 4

The entire way to The Pitbull's prison, Briar kept her feelings to herself. She didn't scream or shout and she didn't cry. She didn't want The Pitbull's men telling him that she was upset or seemed in the least bit worried about being locked up. She didn't want her uncle thinking he'd broken her spirit.

The men brought her to the thirty-ninth floor of The Pitbull's tower. She had been to this floor before, but was surprised to see it had completely changed. Gone were the comfortable couches and low coffee tables, the chandeliers and the velvet curtains. In their place were concrete walls, iron bars and security cameras.

Exiting the lift, the men turned right and marched Briar down a long corridor. At the end they came to a concrete block wall, in which were set two heavy steel doors, side by side.

A guard unlocked one of the doors and booted it open.

"Welcome to your new home," he said, with an ugly smile.

He pushed Briar into the cell, stepped back and slammed the door. The key turned in the lock.

Briar waited until she could no longer hear the men's footsteps in the corridor. Then, she turned to inspect her cell. There wasn't much to inspect. On the floor was a single woollen blanket which she suspected was her bed – there was certainly nothing else soft in the cell. Behind a low partition she found a toilet but no sink. High in the wall was a single round window no larger than a dinner plate. Instead of glass, the window had heavy steel bars.

And that was it. The sum total of her prison cell. There was nothing to look at, no books to read, no one to talk to. There was nothing to do.

Briar felt her emotions well up inside her. It was like a tide she couldn't fight against. The awful pain and sadness of losing her parents, then being sent to live with The Pitbull, her terrible loneliness, her powerlessness. It bubbled up from somewhere deep inside, from a place she'd kept secret. She'd needed to, so that her uncle and his men couldn't sense any weakness in her. She had needed to stay strong to survive.

Briar put her back to the wall and slid down to the floor. The tears came quickly, running freely down her cheeks. She lay on her side and curled into a tight ball, hugging her knees to her chest. Her quiet sobs became louder as finally she let go; all of her pain and suffering now came out and she cried and cried.

Her sobbing eased and she began to feel better. The terrible pain in her heart had lessened, and she was able to properly draw breath. She lay still as the hurt left her, bit by bit. Finally, all was quiet but for the sound of her own breathing.

Briar turned over and rested her head on the cold concrete floor. Her eyes fell on the gap beneath the door and she slid over, her cheek flat to the ground. Now she could see right up the corridor. One of the men had stayed behind and was sitting in a chair at the far end. Otherwise there appeared to be no one else around.

Briar watched the guard for a while. He scratched himself, yawned, then leaned his chair back on the wall and closed his eyes. He was obviously bored. There was little reason for him to guard the cell; it was clear Briar couldn't escape.

Since there was nothing else to do, Briar continued to watch him. After about ten minutes, one of his arms dropped from his lap to dangle by his side. Then, his jaw fell open. He was asleep.

That's when she heard it.

"Are you all right, dear?"

Briar jolted in shock. She listened intently. The voice had been so soft it was barely above a whisper. She wasn't even sure she'd heard it at all; she could just as easily have imagined it. Was she going mad already? She said nothing. In fact, the longer the silence went on, the more foolish she felt. Her mind must indeed be playing tricks on her. But she held her breath, and listened.

"Can you hear me, dear? Are you all right?"

Briar jumped again, but this time she was in no doubt. She hesitated for a moment before answering.

"Hello?" she whispered. "Is somebody there?"

"Oh, hello dear," replied the voice. It was the soft, kind voice of a woman. It immediately made Briar feel better, although she had no idea who it belonged to. "Tell me, dear, did they hurt you? Are you all right?"

"No. I'm fine… I'm just… sad, that's all."

"I know dear, we heard you crying. It nearly broke our hearts."

"We?" said Briar.

"Yes," replied the woman. "My husband and I are in the cell next to yours. I'm afraid we're captives of The Pitbull too."

"Hello, young lady," said the voice of a man. He sounded friendly and cheery, despite his situation.

"Hello," said Briar. "Oh, that's terrible. Are you OK?" She immediately felt more concern for the couple in the next cell than for herself.

"Oh, don't worry about us, dear," replied the woman. "We're just fine. But you must keep your voice down. The young fellow down at the end of the corridor gets a bit agitated if he hears talking. What's your name?"

Briar kept her eye on the guard. "Briar," she whispered. "What are your names?"

"I'm Millicent. And my husband here is Roger."

"Lovely to meet you, Briar," said Roger.

"Nice to meet you too," said Briar. She felt much better already.

"Tell me dear, who are you? Where are your parents?"

Briar felt a hot prickling in the back of her throat. Millicent's kindness made her feel like crying all over again.

"My parents died. The Pitbull is my uncle."

"Oh no! That's terrible!" cried Millicent.

Briar could hear Roger urging her to keep her voice down, but the guard didn't stir.

"What sort of a man puts his own niece in a prison cell? I'm sorry to say this to you, dear – I know he's your uncle – but he's not very nice."

"That's quite all right," replied Briar. "I know he isn't. I feel the same way."

Briar thought for a moment. "Why are you here?" she asked.

Roger mumbled something and Millicent hushed him. "It's a bit of a long story," she said, "but we think it's because our family has upset your uncle."

Suddenly, Briar realised what Millicent was saying. "You're talking about Flynn and Paddy – the boys from the island – aren't you?"

"Yes," replied Millicent with surprise. "They're our grandsons."

CHAPTER 5

"Is this it?" asked Paddy, holding up a tall leafy plant. He had ripped it out of the ground and was examining it, a quizzical look on his face.

Flynn looked over. Their mother had sent them out to collect lion's ear, and so far Paddy had found a dozen plants that were anything but.

Flynn sighed. "No, Paddy. That's not it. That doesn't look remotely like it."

Paddy frowned. "Are you sure? I think it looks a lot like it."

"Except that the leaves are completely different and it doesn't have any flowers on it at all," replied Flynn.

"Oh yeah," replied Paddy. He flung the plant away into the undergrowth and resumed his search.

Their mother had sent them out to find herbs for a poultice for their father, who'd twisted his ankle badly that morning. He'd been carrying an armful of firewood and stepped awkwardly. Their mother said his mind wasn't on the job. She thought he was worried about their grandparents, who still hadn't arrived.

The ankle was badly swollen and he couldn't put any weight on it. He would have to rest it for at least five days, their mother said. The poultice would help speed the healing – she had used it many times on the boys' sprains and bruises.

Eventually, they'd collected enough, and set off towards home. They were almost there, walking back along the beach, when they heard a noise and looked up to see a plane in the distance. In a flash they dropped everything and raised their weapons.

Paddy felt sure he could put an arrow into the engine. But it came in incredibly fast – faster than any plane they had ever seen. It was low, just a few hundred feet above the water, heading directly towards their home. It was a jet, but painted black instead of the usual air force green. The noise was terrific. As it passed above them, they spotted the white dog's head emblazoned on the underside of its wings.

Elton and Iris, who were lying asleep on the beach in a tangle of wings, tails and long scaly legs, woke with a start and sprang into the air, ready to give chase. But even they couldn't have caught the plane. It rocketed inland for a few seconds more before banking hard and climbing quickly into the blue sky. Then it turned for the mainland and was gone.

"I don't like the look of this." said Paddy.

"Look," said Flynn, pointing. A tiny white parachute was drifting slowly down towards the beach. "The plane must have dropped it. I think we're about to find out what it was doing here."

"Oh, this is so bad," said Paddy.

The boys jogged down to the water's edge. The parachute landed in the water and Flynn had to wade in to his waist to fish it out.

Returning to the beach, he and Paddy took a close look at it. Beneath the tiny canopy was a small steel canister with a screw-top lid.

"Should we open it?" said Flynn.

Paddy shrugged. "I don't know."

Flynn gauged its weight. It felt like there was nothing inside. But when he shook it, he heard something rattle.

"Whatever's in it, it's small," he said.

"Open it," said Paddy. "But make sure you hold it away from your face." He took a few steps backwards.

"Thanks," said Flynn, with a grim smile.

The top unscrewed easily. Flynn slowly lifted the lid and looked inside. Something small sat at the bottom. It glistened. He turned the canister over onto his palm. Out fell a tiny ring. It was old – silver, with a single emerald mounted high in a clasp. Flynn gasped, and Paddy recoiled in horror. Both boys recognised the ring immediately: it was their grandmother's.

CHAPTER 6

Briar hadn't talked so much and for so long in what seemed like forever. For the past two years no one had shown the slightest interest in what she had to say. But now, here in a prison cell, whispered beneath two steel doors, her story tumbled out.

She had cried three times already. Millicent and Roger waited patiently for her to stop, and encouraged her to continue.

Briar told them first about her mother – the sweet, kind woman who'd cared not a bit for fancy houses, nice cars and diamond rings, but rather for the natural world and all the wild and wonderful plants and animals that lived in it. She'd been a scientist, and because of her work Briar and her parents had travelled all over the world. Briar was born deep in the Amazon jungle, hundreds of miles from the nearest hospital, during the two years her mother was tasked with discovering the breeding habits of the Amazon river dolphin. Briar had loved hearing her mother tell the story of her birth – how the women of the jungle helped to bring her into the world and took turns caring for her while her mother studied the dolphins.

They'd lived in Madagascar for a year while her mother studied the hissing cockroach, a remarkable insect that hisses loudly after winning an epic cockroach battle. And in Namibia, they'd lived for three months on the edge of a desert, where Briar had helped her mother survey the cheetah population.

Next, Briar told Millicent and Roger about her father, explaining how patient, clever, and funny he was, how content he'd been to roam the world, living in tents and mud huts, travelling on rafts and in the backs of uncomfortable trucks. "As long as I have my family around me, I'm home," he'd say. He could invent anything; able to make the most marvellous things out of very little. In Tanzania, he'd built the villagers a schoolhouse, complete with desks, blackboard, rainwater drinking fountains and composting toilets; in Indonesia, he'd helped the poorest farmers plant their crops and showed them how to build an irrigation system, which meant they'd never have to lug their huge containers of water again.

As Briar grew up, she'd learned the most incredible skills: how to track an animal through long grass; how to extract honey from a tree-top beehive; how to keep safe when surrounded by a pride of lions. It had been a remarkable education, almost never involving a classroom, pens and paper, or computers. Her friends had been the children of remote villages all over the world, and she spoke a little of at least a dozen languages.

But, Briar's life as she'd known it had come to an end two years ago, on a remote road in Norway. They'd been on a rare holiday, staying with a friend of her parents in a little cottage overlooking a dramatic fjord – a kind of finger of the sea which reached far inland. The weather had been frightful. A wild storm had blown in from the ocean, bringing howling wind, snow, and ice – but the cottage couldn't have been cosier. A fire crackled in a wood stove, a pot of stew bubbled on top. They'd played cards and read books and told each other ghost stories.

When the weather cleared a little, Briar's parents had borrowed their friend's car to explore the area. Briar had wanted to check out the beach at the bottom of the fjord so she'd stayed behind.

It was the last time she ever saw her parents. Their car hit a large patch of ice, skidded, and began to spin. Briar had created an awful film of it in her mind. She could almost feel the sensation as the car twisted and slid on the black ice. For a moment, she imagined it was frictionless, peaceful, until the car reached the side of the road and the wheels bit into the gravel, flipping it over and over as it rolled down a bank. Both of them had been killed instantly.

Millicent cried out at this point in the story, and whispered her concern and sympathy beneath the steel door. Briar's voice wavered as she tried to hold back the tears.

Briar had thought life couldn't get any worse, until she was sent to live with her uncle. As her only living relative, he'd reluctantly agreed to be her guardian, on the condition that all of Briar's parents' money and possessions were given to him. The family lawyer had refused his request, but The Pitbull had put a dozen of his own lawyers on the job. Neither Briar nor her lawyer had the will or the money to fight him and Briar had been far too sad to care what happened to her parents' money.

Her memories of going to live at The Pitbull's home were vague. It had seemed an endless, soulless warren of rooms and corridors, with no personality – no family photographs, no children's drawings, no books, no music. She realised there was little in his life other than his businesses, which were mostly illegal.

She was told to join him for dinner, where they'd sit at opposite ends of a long marble table. He'd rarely spoken, or even looked at her. He'd seemed intent on eating as fast as he could – the sound of him chewing his meat had driven Briar mad. On finishing his meal, he'd roughly push his plate away, stand up and walk out. It had been as far from a normal family meal as it was possible to be.

After about a week, Briar had begun to explore his enormous house, and was shocked to come across The Pitbull's private zoo and its collection of deadly and dangerous animals. It was clear that The Pitbull, like her mother, had a fascination with animals.

But where she'd loved to see them in their natural environment, he liked to control them, to capture and lock them up. They were all underfed, miserable, and lonely. That was the way The Pitbull liked it; he wanted them to growl and snap whenever he walked past their cages.

But the animals had an effect on Briar that The Pitbull couldn't have foreseen. She spent more and more time in the zoo, secretly feeding them pieces of meat stolen from the vast kitchen, or saved from one of her meals. The chefs didn't notice the odd sausage or lamb chop going missing. Briar had visited every day; sometimes twice a day, sneaking down to the zoo, the meat wrapped in paper and hidden beneath her clothes. Taking care to stay away from the dozens of security cameras around the zoo, Briar had pushed the food through the bars, where it was eagerly wolfed down by the starving creatures.

As the animals' ravenous hunger was satisfied, they stopped snarling at Briar. They came to realise she meant them no harm, and was trying to help them in whatever way she could. Soon she could lean against the cage walls, a tiger or leopard just inches away through the bars, so close that Briar could feel the warmth of their bodies. She spoke to them in a soft voice, or sang to them.

It had been there, surrounded by the animals of The Pitbull's zoo, that Briar finally made peace with herself and accepted the loss of her parents. The presence of the animals made her less lonely, and gave her the much-needed company she longed for. But she also hated her uncle for locking them up, and vowed one day to free them if she could.

When Briar finished speaking, there was silence for a short time. Then she heard Millicent's comforting voice.

"That's the saddest story I've heard in a long time. I wish I could give you a hug, but I can't – so I'm placing my hand on the wall between our cells. Put your hand up there too."

Briar shifted a little so she could reach the wall, and placed her hand against it.

"Close your eyes," said Millicent.

Briar closed her eyes.

"Now, listen very carefully," said Millicent. "Everything is going to be all right... it's all going to work out just fine. Do you believe me?"

Briar smiled. She believed her. "Yes."

"Good girl. Now, don't you ever forget it."

Down the corridor, the guard stirred, woken by the sound of soft voices. He stood and listened, then crept silently towards the cells. As he got closer, he heard it again – the prisoners were speaking to each other!

"SILENCE!" he screamed. "If I hear any of you again there'll be trouble!"

For a moment there wasn't a sound. Then he heard the old woman's voice.

"Oh, hush up young man!"

The guard raged and shouted. He kicked the old couple's door, but he didn't go inside. Eventually, he calmed down. Hearing nothing more, he returned to his post. Inside her cell, Briar giggled. She moved to the far side of the room and curled up onto the blanket. Within minutes, she was sound asleep.

CHAPTER 7

"It's there somewhere, I know it is."

Despite the seriousness of the situation, Flynn and Paddy couldn't help laughing at their father.

"Are you absolutely sure? How on earth do you lose something so big?" said Paddy, which set the two boys off again.

"And, how on earth have you kept it a secret for all this time?" added Flynn.

The brothers were standing thigh-deep in a stream, peering into the thicket of trees overhanging the bank. Their father, on makeshift crutches, his foot heavily bandaged, hobbled along the opposite bank yelling instructions.

"Don't be smart," he said. "Just keep looking.Perhaps you should split up – Flynn, you go upstream and Paddy you go downstream. Check behind every tree."

The boys did as they were told. Paddy wandered off around the bend in the stream, half-heartedly poking through the bushes at the edge. Flynn waded upstream against the current. He battled his way through the branches of a tree that had recently toppled into the water, pushing hard through the thick curtain of leaves. By the time he made it through, his hair had turned silver with the silk of a dozen spiderwebs.

Beyond the tree, along the bank, was a wall of green foliage. Flynn sighed – this could take a while. Then, something caught his eye. There was something unusual about a branch that was poking horizontally out from the undergrowth. The end was rounded and smooth. As he got closer, he saw strands of flax hanging from it. Closer still, and he realised the flax passed through a hole in the end of the branch. Now that he could see it more clearly, it had the look of an old flax rope! It was frayed and rotted, but he could clearly see the interwoven strands. Hurriedly, he scrambled up the bank and forced his way between the trees, snapping the branches in order to get a proper look. There, sitting in the forest, was his father's boat!

When the boys, white-faced with worry, had rushed back to the house clutching their grandmother's ring, their poor mother had cried out in alarm. She'd begun to shake all over, and had to be comforted by their father, whose jaw clenched with anger.

Poor Ada hadn't understood what was going on, and kept asking if their grandmother had arrived and why she'd given the boys her ring.

Eventually, their mother had pulled herself together. She and their father had looked at each other for a long time, saying nothing.

"What is it?" Paddy asked. He couldn't bear the silence.

"You boys are going to have to go to the mainland," said their mother.

For once in his life, Paddy had nothing to say. He sat in stunned silence, his thoughts spinning and twisting in a hundred directions.

No one had ever before suggested leaving the island, not for any reason. Now it seemed there was no choice but to do exactly that.

Finally, Flynn found his voice. "But how?" he asked.

"In my boat," said their father.

Flynn and Paddy's mouths had dropped open. They'd spoken in unison, their surprise overcoming their worry.

"You have a boat?"

It took the boys more than an hour to hack away the trees and vines that had grown up around their father's boat. It was hard, hot, exhausting work. Their father had to watch from across the stream. Finally, they were ready to attempt to haul it out of the trees.

It was too large and heavy for the boys on their own, so Flynn ran a rope from the bow right across the stream, while Paddy fetched their faithful horse, Clappers. Flynn tied a rope harness around her chest and neck while she stood patiently. Finally, they were ready. Paddy re-crossed the stream and stood, axe in hand, in case he needed to chop through any final vines or trees clinging onto the boat.

"Ready?" called Flynn.

"All set," replied Paddy.

Flynn urged Clappers forward.

After the initial heave to get it moving, the boat suddenly broke free and slid out of the trees and down the bank. Paddy saw his opportunity and leapt on board, emerging from the trees like a Viking standing on a longboat.

"Captain Paddy reporting for duty!" he yelled, saluting Flynn and his father, who laughed at him.

As it glided out onto the clear water of the stream, the boys got a decent look at their father's sailing boat.

Here's your first opportunity to use the **AR Reads** app on your device (if you haven't downloaded it, find out how at the beginning of this book. If you have, make sure it's the latest version by downloading any updates).

Simply start up the app, then point the device at this page and check out Flynn and Paddy's father's boat! If you don't have a device – don't worry – just read on!

It was a trimaran – it had three hulls. There was a large central hull with smaller, stabilising hulls either side, all connected by two strong beams fixed across them. The central hull was more than twenty feet long, and at its centre, over two feet wide. The pole Flynn had seen sticking out of the bushes was the bowsprit, where a rope would be tied to stabilise the mast. At the front and back – the bow and stern – this hull was covered over with rough planks, creating two tiny covered rooms. Between them was the open part of the cockpit, which housed nothing more than two simple seats. A paddle was jammed beneath them. A long pole reached from the cockpit to the stern of the boat. This was the tiller, for steering the boat. The rudder itself had been removed and stowed inside the room at the back. The mast and boom were lashed to the cross beams.

It was clear the trimaran hadn't been used in a long time; their father guessed it was fifteen years since he'd last laid eyes on it. The flax ropes had rotted away and the entire structure was loose. The sail was nowhere to be seen. The timber, however, was as good as the day it was built – their father had covered it with many layers of palm leaves to keep the rain off.

"I remember that in a fair breeze she used to cream along at a decent clip," he said, which made Flynn and Paddy laugh again.

"Is that right, Captain Cook?" said Paddy cheekily.

"Why did you stop using it?" asked Flynn.

"I had no need of it," replied their father. "I had a little canoe that I used for fishing, and your grandparents would bring anything we needed from the mainland in their yacht. Besides, it was difficult to handle on my own. Do you think you could sail it?"

Paddy snorted. "In our sleep! Easy peasy!"

Flynn looked thoughtful. "I think so. Depending on how fast it goes, and how favourable the wind and swell are, it should take us three or maybe four days to get to the mainland. I think we can do it."

Their father's face creased with worry.

"You must do it," he said. "Your grandparents' lives may depend on it."

CHAPTER 8

Two days later, early in the morning, Flynn and Paddy stood on the shore of Home Lagoon, holding the bow of their father's boat into the wind. A fresh breeze blew from the east, making the new sail flap and crack like a whip. It was little more than a dozen canvas sacks sewn together by their mother, but it was as strong as she could make it. A second sail was stashed inside the main hull. The mainsheet – a plaited flax rope attached to the boom – flicked to and fro in the wind.

Inside, packed fore and aft, was plenty of food, water, bedding, and warm clothing. Extra rope was stored in the stern. Near the bow, tied to the deck, were bundles of bamboo lashed together. These had been made by their father, and would serve as floatation devices if anything went wrong.

Everything had been strengthened, reinforced, and tightened – the mast, boom, and rigging were as strong as they could make them.

Their father had spent the past two days showing them how to navigate using the sun and stars, a pocket watch and a strange-looking device called a sextant. At certain times of the day, they were to take a bearing on the sun or stars to ensure they were heading in the right direction. He showed them how to plot their course on a map.

They were ready. Their mother stood quietly on the beach, looking sick with worry. Poor Ada clung tightly to her. Their father's face was ashen – they'd never seen him look so concerned. The only carefree creature was Coco, their dog, who leapt about barking and licking the boys' legs. She obviously thought she was going on an adventure too.

"Sorry, girl," said Flynn. "You have to stay home and look after everyone."

Their mother suddenly put down Ada, waded into the water and placed her hands on the brothers' cheeks.

"Listen to me. We love you so much. Please don't take any risks. Remember – as soon as you arrive you're to go straight to the police station and tell them everything. Don't go anywhere else. Don't you dare go near The Pitbull."

"We won't. Promise," replied Paddy.

"Try not to worry," said Flynn. "We can do this. Everything will be fine."

As the boys cast off, they searched the sky above their home one last time, but it was empty. When the plane that dropped their grandmother's ring had gone, Elton and Iris had taken to the air, speeding off in the direction of Mother's Knee Hill, perhaps frightened by the terrific noise of the jet. The boys hadn't seen them since.

"Be careful!" called their father.

As the boys passed over the reef, the only sounds were the roar of the surf and the distant barking of Coco back on the beach. It dawned on them that they were leaving the island for the first time and it made them feel sad, nervous, frightened and excited in equal measure.

"Come on," said Flynn. "Let's get going."

They got to work. Paddy hauled in the mainsheet while Flynn guided the boat through the deepest part of the outer reef, where the waves passed without breaking. As soon as they were clear of the island, they turned due west and trimmed the sails. The boat responded magnificently, picking up speed until foam trailed from the hulls in the water. Paddy climbed out on the upwind hull to provide ballast and the boat fairly raced along.

"This is awesome!" he called to Flynn, who despite his worry was also enjoying the sensation of speed.

This boat was much faster than their grandparents' yacht.

"Want to put up the other sail?" Flynn asked Paddy, who nodded enthusiastically.

Before long, the boys had the foresail up too, and the boat leapt away, gaining an extra couple of knots. Flynn quickly became used to the way the trimaran responded to little movements of the rudder, and Paddy kept a constant eye on the sail, ensuring it was filled with wind at all times. They tried a few gibes, flipping the boom and sail to the opposite side, and found they could perform the manoeuvre with ease.

The boys spent the rest of the day familiarising themselves with their boat and practising raising and dropping sails, tacking and gybing.

As the sky began to redden with the setting sun, Paddy looked back at the island. To his surprise, he could no longer see it – it was already well below the horizon.

"Look Flynn!" he shouted, a note of panic in his voice.

Fear swelled in his stomach. They had never travelled this far from home, never been out of sight of the island – even on their grandparents' yacht. It was a constant presence in their lives, and now that it was gone, Paddy felt lost and alone out on the vast, darkening ocean.

"We'll be all right. Don't worry," said Flynn, but he sounded unsure.

They were going to The Pitbull's land. They were losing their home advantage. They were, he realised, literally out of their depth.

Suddenly, above the wind and the sound of the sea, the boys heard a familiar noise.

"*Squeee!*"

"Lightning!" yelled Paddy, leaping to his feet. They looked up into the darkening sky. The sound had come from the direction of the island, where the moon had begun to rise. "*Squeee!*"

Their pet falcon called twice more, high above the boat. Then, he swooped down and landed on the end of the bowsprit. There, he wobbled about unsteadily, and fixed the boys with a solemn stare. He looked as though he was terribly upset with the boys for leaving the island, which made them both laugh.

"You crazy bird!" said Paddy. "How did you find us?"

Flynn shook his head. "We need to send him home again. He can't come with us."

Paddy realised Flynn was right. The sea – and the city – were no places for a falcon. With heavy hearts, the brothers tried to shoo him away, but he wouldn't budge.

"Go away!" yelled Flynn. "Go home!"

Paddy handed the mainsheet to Flynn and shinnied out along the bowsprit, where he prodded at Lightning. Eventually, the falcon took off.

Only to land on top of the mast.

"*Squeee!*"

For a while Paddy tried scaring the falcon away by waving the paddle at him, but Lightning simply took off and hovered above the boat until Paddy got tired or bored, then landed on the mast again.

"It's hopeless," he finally said to Flynn. "He's not going anywhere."

Flynn agreed. "Leave him be. It's actually kind of nice to have him along."

Lightning seemed to sense the boys' decision, because no sooner had they made it than he swooped down to Flynn's shoulder, where he promptly went to sleep. The boys laughed, and Flynn stroked his soft belly.

"What's for dinner, Paddy?" asked Flynn. "I can't possibly make it, because I'll wake up Lightning."

Paddy smiled. "OK. Coming right up."

CHAPTER 9

Briar awoke with a start, her cheek cold against the concrete floor. Her hip ached from where she'd been lying on it – the blanket didn't provide much padding. She turned over onto the other hip and tried to close her eyes again. The trick was to fall asleep before it began to ache. But the moon had risen and was shining straight through the high round window onto her face, bathing the cell in a milky light.

Now wide awake, she sat up and stretched. She felt a panicky impulse to shout and beat the walls, but fought it back. She thought of Millicent's voice, telling her that everything would be all right.

Briar had no idea what time it was. It might be midnight or five o'clock in the morning, she had no way of knowing. She ran her hands through her hair, and her fingers snagged on something. A hair pin. She pulled it out and laid it on the ground while she combed her hair with her fingers. It was already in a terrible tangle.

Tidying up her hair somehow made her feel better. It mattered that she didn't give up hope. As she worked out the knots, she stared at the hair pin on the floor. A silly idea slowly worked its way into her mind. Picking up the pin, Briar shuffled to the concrete block wall separating her cell from Millicent and Roger's. She began to scratch at it with the pin. Within a few minutes, the plastic blob on the end of the steel had worn away against the rough concrete. She began to etch her name into the block. It was slow going, but by the light of the moon she could see she was making progress.

She was planning to write 'Briar was here'. For some reason, the silliness of it cheered her up.

It took her fifteen minutes to scratch the letters 'Bri' and she was just about to start on the 'a' when a thought struck her.

Briar held the hair pin firmly between her fingers and pushed it into the mortar – the thin layer of cement between the concrete blocks. To her surprise, it yielded slightly, and she saw a tiny stream of white dust fall away from the wall. She pushed harder, then looked closely, straining to see in the dim light. Yes! There was a definite mark from the clip!

Briar could feel her excitement mounting as she set to work. She scratched furiously for a few minutes, then stopped. She had to think. She was rushing into this. Was it wise? What was she hoping to do?

She sat back and stared at the wall for a long time. Then, slowly and deliberately, she went back to work. She chose one of the lowest blocks on the wall, and began to scratch away at the mortar.

Every now and again, when a pile of dust had collected on the ground, she swept it up with her hands and put it on the windowsill of the high round window. There, she spread it out evenly, so it wouldn't be noticed by the guard. In this way, she worked through the rest of the night.

As the light of dawn began to filter through the window, Briar stopped. She had straightened the pin to be able to dig deeper into the wall, and reckoned she was about halfway through. The rest would have to be done from Millicent and Roger's side.

She gathered up about a tablespoon of the white mortar dust, pushed it into the centre of her palm, and mustering as much saliva as she could, spat on it half a dozen times. When she figured she had enough, she mixed it into a paste with her finger and began to push it back into the exposed gap around the block. It took just a couple of minutes to smear it right around. She sat back to take a look. It was slightly darker than the surrounding bricks, but already she could see that when it dried out a little it would be impossible to spot.

CHAPTER 10

After a meal of bread and goat's cheese, Paddy crawled into the tiny room in the bow, curled up, and went to sleep. They would do two-hour shifts through the night.

Flynn took a bearing on the sextant, then fetched a blanket and wrapped himself in it. He found a comfortable nook to sit in and enjoyed the sail. An hour and a half passed, and then the wind suddenly died away completely. The boat was barely moving, and the surface of the sea turned into a glossy sheet of black glass.

"Oh, come on," hissed Flynn, frustrated at the lack of progress. He was anxious to get to the mainland.

As he spoke, there came a mighty *whoosh*, and seconds later Flynn was showered by a fine mist of salt water. Beside him, perched on the rudder pole, Lightning gave an alarmed "*squeee*" and leapt into the air, fluttering upwards into the darkness. Confused, Flynn sat bolt upright and reached for his slingshot. Beside the boat, an enormous black hulk had breached the surface of the sea. It was a whale! Then, from the other side of the boat, Flynn heard another *whoosh*, and turned to see a second whale spouting water from its blowhole.

"Paddy," shouted Flynn. "Come and see!"

"What is it?" Paddy's voice was thick with sleep as he crawled out of his bed and clambered unsteadily to his feet. "Is it my turn? Why are you yelling?"

Flynn gasped. More and more whales were surfacing all around them, shooting moonlit columns of spray into the air.

"Oh. Wow," said Paddy, sitting down. He was suddenly wide awake.

The whales surfaced and dived all around them for almost half an hour. The brothers were entranced. They could hear them clicking and squealing to each other. Occasionally, one would lift its tail high in the air and slap it down, drenching the boys. They didn't mind at all – it was a wonderful display of such huge and graceful animals.

Then, just like that, they were gone, diving back into the inky black depths of the ocean. Lightning landed back on the boat. The brothers high-fived and hugged each other, delighted to have witnessed such an incredible sight.

Then, as if on cue, the breeze sprang up again, filling the sail and speeding them on their way.

"Right. Back to bed," said Paddy, making for the cabin.

"Hey… not so fast, brother," said Flynn.

He pulled out their father's watch. "It's your turn."

"What? Already?" Paddy couldn't believe it.

Flynn handed him the watch.

"Take a bearing. Set a course," he said, before crawling into his own bed. "Don't fall asleep."

Paddy grumbled. "Good night to you too."

By the time Paddy's shift was over, the wind was blowing a steady twenty knots. In the time it took to drop the foresail and put a reef in the mainsail, it had risen to thirty. The sea was also rising, with wind chop created by the freshening breeze. Despite the smaller sail area, the boat rocketed along before the wind.

Paddy crawled into his bed and tried to sleep, but the movement of the boat made him crash into one side of the hull, then the other. He was fed up. He pulled on a jumper and came back out on deck, sitting miserably beside Flynn.

"Fun's over," he said.

"Looks like it," replied Flynn. "At least we're going fast."

Flynn was right. The boat was travelling at incredible speed, which only increased as the wind rose to forty knots, then fifty. They surfed down the front of the huge swells that had developed, while Flynn wrestled with the rudder, trying to keep the boat travelling at an angle down the waves so they didn't nose-dive at the bottom.

Paddy put another reef in the sail, a risky exercise in the heaving ocean. It made the sail area even smaller, but it made little difference. The wind was blowing so hard they barely needed a sail at all.

Now, the sea was a different beast entirely. Great black lumps of ocean rose up behind them, occasionally cresting and breaking, releasing an avalanche of white water down the face of the wave. Flynn, still on the rudder and rapidly tiring, tried everything to avoid them, putting the boat into wild gybes to get out of the path of breaking waves. Paddy worked the mainsheet, trying to release the tremendous gusts threatening to send the boat catapulting end over end.

Occasionally they were caught in a breaking wave, and the boat would careen crazily off to one side. Twice the boat broached, heeling over so far that the rudder came out of the water, sending the boat into a frightening skid. The boys held on for dear life!

There was now no way they could take a bearing. Clouds covered the moon and stars. And besides, the boat was flying about so violently, it took all their effort just to hold on. They squinted, trying to see through the driving rain, and had to yell to make themselves heard. The howling wind screamed through the rigging, threatening to tear the sail from the mast. If they had been able to, they would have taken the sail down entirely, but it was far too dangerous to attempt. Luckily, their mother had made a strong sail, and it held fast.

The boat, however, was a different story. Flynn could see that the lashings holding the cross beams to the three hulls were beginning to loosen under the tremendous strain. There was little he could do about it until the sea calmed down. He said nothing to Paddy until it was clearly obvious to him, too. The boat had lost its rigidness, and was becoming more and more difficult to control.

At last, a thin streak of light began to appear in the east. The wind still blew fiercely, but daylight took away some of the terror – at least they could tell when one of the giant waves racing up behind them was about to break.

But, by now, the boat was seriously damaged. Paddy retrieved one of the spare ropes to strengthen the lashings, but it was impossible, as well as being incredibly dangerous. He gave up after a few minutes.

"Grab the bamboo packs," said Flynn, a grim look on his face.

Paddy untied the two packs, making his way back to the cockpit like a crab crawling across a rock.

"The boat's going to break up, isn't it?" he said.

"Yes."

There was nothing to do but wait. The boys sat side by side, clutching the bamboo packs, waiting for the inevitable. The boat sliced through the water at a scarcely believable speed. At the end of each crazy surf down the face of a wave it skewed wildly as it bottomed out in the trough. The whole boat flexed and bent, and Paddy and Flynn watched as, one by one, the lashings snapped and began to unravel.

"Get ready," said Flynn, and the two boys crouched in the cockpit, ready to fling themselves overboard.

Paddy looked over at Flynn.

"Is this it?" he asked. His eyes were wild with terror.

Flynn looked at his brother and smiled.

"Remember what Mum and Dad always say when we go to bed? 'You've got what it takes; never give up'. Don't forget that."

Paddy nodded. "OK. I won't."

He looked out at the sea. Huge grey-green peaks of water stretched out behind them like a mountain range. Back there, somewhere, was their island.

There was an almighty crack from the boat and it gave an awful shudder. Paddy felt it travel through his own body. He couldn't bear to look at where the sound had come from. Instead, he lifted his eyes to the horizon. He felt the boat rise as a truly enormous wave caught them from behind. He heard the roar of it breaking, and braced himself for the impact and the deluge of water that would finally destroy the boat. The moment before it struck, just as they rose to the top of the wave, Paddy got a fleeting glimpse of the horizon in front of them. In the distance, through the driving sea spray and torrential rain, he saw a dark smudge. Land.

CHAPTER 11

"Pssst. Psssst."

The sun streamed down through the trees as Roger cycled his old bicycle down the avenue. It was a beautiful autumn day, and leaves the colour of rust and sunsets fluttered down from the oak trees to settle on the road. He could smell the turning of the season.

"Psssssssst."

There was that sound again! He looked down at his front tyre and to his dismay saw that it was rapidly going flat. A flat tyre! What a bother!

"Pssst. Roger… Millicent!"

With a start, Roger awoke from his dream to find that he wasn't cycling down a sunny avenue at all, but rather was imprisoned in a cold concrete cell. He sat up, and pain knifed through his body. Every joint and muscle ached from lying on the cold, hard floor.

"Pssst. Wake up!" came the voice again.

"Millicent. Wake up," cried Roger. Despite his stiffness, he shuffled quickly over to the steel door and put his cheek against the ground. A quick look at the guard told him he was fast asleep.

"Briar… is that you?"

"Oh Roger, thank goodness you heard me. I have something to tell you."

Roger was joined by Millicent at the cell door and together they listened eagerly as Briar explained her night's work.

"The trouble is, the pin won't reach any further through the wall. You'll have to do the rest from your side. Then at least we can talk to each other properly," said Briar.

"That would be wonderful," exclaimed Millicent loudly, forgetting the guard, who stirred, then fell back asleep.

"Quiet, Millicent, for goodness sake," hissed Roger. "There's just one problem. How are you going to get the pin to us?"

"I've been working on that," came Briar's reply.

"I've unravelled a piece of cotton from my T-shirt. It's about two feet long, which should be enough to reach to your door. I tied the pin to one end, and if I hold on to the other, keeping the cotton tight, then give the hairpin a hard flick it should swing around in an arc and end up under your door. Shall I try it?"

"Great idea," Roger whispered. "Give it a go."

Holding the end of the cotton at the side of the door closest to Roger and Millicent's cell, Briar stretched it taut and placed the pin on the ground.

She flicked it – hard. It flew under the door, travelled three-quarters of the way around the arc, then came to halt.

"Not bad, but I'll have to try again," she whispered.

Briar tried again and again, but each time the pin fell at least six inches short of Roger and Millicent's door.

"Bother!" said Roger. "I can see it, but there's no way to reach it."

Suddenly, there was a shout from the guard, who came running down the corridor. Briar could see his heavy black boots thumping along the ground as he approached.

"I told you not to talk to each other!" he yelled, then he kicked both doors as hard as he could. "You'll get nothing for breakfast!" he bellowed. "And the next time I hear a noise from any of you you'll get nothing for a week!"

Briar recoiled, shrinking away from the violence of the man outside. It was only when he stalked back to his post that she looked under the door and saw that the cotton was gone.

Next door, Millicent held something up for her husband to see. The guard's heavy boots had struck the pin, sending it spinning under the door and into their cell.

CHAPTER 12

"Try this on for size, sir."

The Pitbull laid his hand on the velvet cushion. The jeweller's hand shook as he gently eased the signet ring onto The Pitbull's pinky finger. He was obviously scared out of his wits.

"Quickly!" snapped The Pitbull.

Once the ring was on, he shooed the man away so he could admire it in peace. It was huge, and heavy of course, being solid gold. Engraved in the top was the dog's head, its teeth bared in a ferocious snarl.

"Get back here," he commanded. "Melt the wax."

The jeweller hurried back with a candle and a ruby red stick of wax. He lit the candle and held the wax over it until it began to drip, catching the melted wax on a page of the finest-quality writing paper.

"Now sir, if you'll press the ring firmly down into the wax…"

"I know what to do," spat The Pitbull.

He made a fist and pushed the ring into the cooling wax, holding it there for a count of ten. Then he pulled it away and admired the dog's head imprinted into the seal.

"Good. You may go," he said to the jeweller.

"Sir – what about payment, sir? Will you be paying by cash or…"

"What?" growled The Pitbull. "What did you say?"

"Or will I send you the bill?"

The Pitbull looked at the jeweller like he was something unpleasant stuck to the bottom of his shoe.

"Your payment? Your payment is that I don't burn your business to the ground. How about that?"

The jeweller's eyes bulged.

"Yes sir. That would be wonderful, sir. Thank you very much." He scurried from the room.

The Pitbull smiled. He took off the ring and held it up to the light. It really was a handsome piece. He slid it back onto his finger.

Then he was struck by a disturbing thought. The ring – the old woman's ring! Perhaps he shouldn't have sent it to the island – it was too much, too extreme! He hadn't thought it through properly. He needed to move quickly, before the brothers reached the mainland.

He yelled at the top of his lungs for his men, who came running from all directions and stood to attention before him. He barked out his orders.

"I want six men sent to watch every police station in the city. Day and night. Sooner or later the brothers will turn up at one of them. I want them caught and brought to me. Go! Get out of my sight!"

As the men left, The Pitbull congratulated himself. He had set the trap – properly this time. All he had to do now was wait.

CHAPTER 13

Flynn and Paddy loved the sea like no other children on earth, but right now they'd had quite enough of it. The wind and rain had calmed down, but great slabs of water still rose and fell around them. The land seemed no closer, despite the boys kicking towards it for almost four hours.

Lightning, meanwhile, had flown off towards the mainland as soon as the boat had broken up and disappeared beneath the waves. Every hour or so he returned to the boys and hovered above them, crying out in distress, before flying away again. The boys realised he was making sure they were swimming in the right direction.

"My bamboo pack is breaking up," said Paddy. Over the past hour its lashing had loosened under the constant battering from the waves.

"Mine too," replied Flynn. "We'd best just relax for a while and gather our strength, because when they're gone we're going to have to swim."

Paddy was silent for a few moments until he rose on a swell and caught sight of the land once more. "Reckon we can make it?"

"Course we can," replied Flynn. "Easy."

The boys bobbed in the turbulent water, each lost in his thoughts. Then Paddy spoke.

"What should we have for lunch?"

Flynn couldn't help but laugh, despite the seriousness of their situation. Here they were, miles from land, and his brother was cracking jokes. He couldn't think of anyone else he'd rather be lost at sea with.

"I was thinking seafood," he said. "With extra salt."

Paddy grinned, and was just about to say something when his jaw dropped open and his face drained of colour.

"What's wrong?" asked Flynn in a panic. Had Paddy spotted a shark?

Paddy looked grim. "Ready for a long swim?" He lifted his hands out of the water. In each he was holding a bamboo length. More popped up all around him. His floatation pack had broken apart.

All the years of spear fishing and diving for lobsters, scallops, and clams had turned the brothers into superb swimmers, but they had never set themselves a challenge like the one the ocean now had in store for them. Gathering as many of the bamboo lengths as they could, they stuffed them inside their shirts for extra floatation and then tucked their shirts into their belts. Flynn's pack still held together, and he tied it to his belt and towed it along behind him.

Then, they swam.

They swam freestyle, then breaststroke. Occasionally they flipped onto their backs and rested, sucking in lungfuls of air. Hour after hour they kept it up – freestyle, breaststroke, rest; freestyle, breaststroke, rest. The clouds cleared away and the sun came out, burning their faces and lips. They became dehydrated – the salt water was like a kind of torture; they could hold it in their mouths but couldn't drink it.

The sun made its way across the sky and the light began to fade. Still they swam. They had made good progress, but were becoming increasingly exhausted.

"Stop," Paddy said. "I need to rest." He flipped onto his back, and Flynn could see that he was shivering and in a bad way. Flynn went to grab his floatation pack, intending to stuff more of the tubes into Paddy's shirt to keep him afloat, but to his dismay, it was gone! It must have broken apart and the bamboo floated away. He cursed himself for his carelessness.

Flynn steeled himself. "Paddy, look at me."

Paddy trod water and turned towards his brother. His eyes were sunken and his lips swollen with sunburn and seawater. He looked awful.

"We didn't come all this way to fail here," said Flynn. "Everyone is relying on us, and we're not going to let them down. The Pitbull is responsible for this and I don't know about you, but I want to see him behind bars. So, you're going to keep swimming, and you're not going to stop. You're not going to rest again until your feet touch land. Do you hear me?" Flynn's voice had risen to a shout.

Paddy set his jaw and nodded and Flynn saw the anger flare in his eyes. They must use that anger to extract the last bit of energy from their bodies.

Once more, the boys flipped onto their stomachs and swam. The sun went down and the moon rose once more, and still they swam. Flynn stayed close to Paddy, nudging him from time to time to let him know he needed to change direction.

Paddy had fallen into a trance-like state that alarmed Flynn. Paddy was barely aware of what he was doing, but still he put one arm in front of the other, and Flynn could only keep him heading in the right direction. He himself began to feel light-headed, and found he was having trouble concentrating. Once, when he looked up, Paddy was nowhere to be seen! Flynn had swum off in a different direction and had forgotten to keep checking for his brother. Luckily, he found him in the darkness and raced back alongside him.

The hours passed as if in a dream. Then, all of a sudden, Flynn felt his body being lifted, as though by an invisible hand. He was used to the rise and fall of passing swells, but this was different. Up and up he went, and he flailed in panic, feeling for Paddy with an outstretched arm. He grabbed his brother's shirt and held on. He lifted his head to see what was happening, but was blinded by spray. For a moment he felt suspended, weightless. Then the world exploded with a violence he could scarcely believe. He was tossed about like a rag doll, end over end, and driven down into the depths. Paddy was ripped from his grasp.

For a long time, Flynn tumbled and twisted deep under the inky black water. He couldn't even tell which way was up. Then, finally, the wave passed over and released its grip on him. Opening his eyes underwater, Flynn made out the ghostly light of the moon, and kicked up towards it. His lungs burned for oxygen. Thankfully, he broke the surface, and gasped in a deep breath of air.

BOOM! Another huge swell smashed down, driving Flynn under again, rolling and tumbling him over and over, before finally letting him go. Another quick gasp for air, then – RUMBLE – a wall of white water mowed him down again. The water was so full of bubbles, his panicked strokes could find little purchase, and he struggled to reach the surface. Finally, he made it, taking a deep breath and willing himself to stay calm while three or four more lines of white water washed over him. Thankfully, each was slightly less powerful than the last.

Then, wonder of wonders, Flynn's foot touched something. Solid ground! He had reached the beach! He stood up and waded in as lines of white water washed past him, occasionally knocking him over.

At last, he stood on the shore. He looked up and down the beach, but in the darkness it was impossible to see much. The moon had disappeared behind a cloud and he could see no more than about twenty yards either side of him. He ran along the hard sand, first one way, then the other. Paddy was nowhere to be seen! Flynn cried out in rage and panic, and continued to run backwards and forwards along the beach, searching. Finally, he stopped, sank to his knees and beat his fists upon the sand. He looked out at the raging sea and cursed it at the top of his lungs.

The moon reappeared from behind the clouds, and the beach was illuminated. Flynn heard Lightning's faint call over the roar of the waves. He couldn't see the falcon, but could roughly judge the direction his cries were coming from. He was hovering out over the water, perhaps a hundred yards down the beach from where Flynn stood.

Flynn took off, running hard through the shallows. He scanned the surf as he ran, and at last he saw a dark shape against the white foam of an oncoming wave. Yelling, he sprinted out into the deeper water. It was Paddy!

Flynn hauled him out of the water. He was unresponsive, his head lolling to the side. In one movement, Flynn threw him onto his shoulder in a fireman's lift. His fear gave him incredible strength. He waded to the beach and gently laid Paddy down on the sand. Anxiously he searched his brother's face, looking for signs of life.

Then, incredibly, wonderfully, Paddy coughed. His body convulsed. Flynn turned him onto his side and he coughed some more and then vomited – nothing but mouthfuls of seawater.

When the vomiting and coughing stopped, Flynn helped Paddy to sit up. He opened his eyes and smiled at Flynn.

"I guess this means we made it?" he said.

Flynn smiled. "Yeah. We made it. Just."

"Did I win?" asked Paddy.

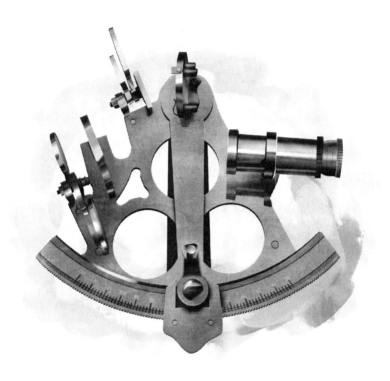

Here's your second opportunity to use the **AR Reads** app on your device.

Simply start up the app, then point the device at this page and check out Flynn and Paddy's perilous journey across the ocean. If you don't have a device – don't worry – just read on!

CHAPTER 14

At about three o'clock in the morning, the mortar cement deep between the concrete blocks suddenly yielded to the hairpin in Roger's hand. He was through! It was all he could do to keep quiet – he wanted to shout to the rooftops. Instead, he made do with some silent fist pumps and a wide grin.

Roger had shooed Millicent away from the wall hours before. She needed to rest, and he was determined to complete the job himself. Now she was sound asleep, and he saw that she was holding onto the finger on her left hand, where her ring should be. It had taken all of his self control to keep quiet when The Pitbull's men had wrenched it off her finger.

For the next hour, Roger worked his way around the block, scratching out the last of the mortar. He experienced a little thrill of satisfaction as each tiny fragment of the cement chipped away.

Finally, he was finished. He stood on tiptoes to look out of the window, but there was no sign of the sunrise yet so he sat down in the darkness and waited. He was far too excited to sleep. Just when he was considering waking his wife, she spoke, making him jump.

"Well? Is it done?"

Roger clasped his hands together in glee. "Yes. I think so. I mean, I haven't tried to move the block, but I'm through all the way around."

"OK. Let's wait until it's almost morning and then we'll try to move it. Come over here and keep me warm."

Roger and Millicent lay together in the darkness, whispering softly to each other.

"Are you all right? Are you frightened?" Roger asked.

"No," replied Millicent. "We'll get out of here somehow. What does The Pitbull want with a couple of old people like us? And surely he won't keep his own niece locked up for long?"

But they both knew that he might do exactly that. And there could be far worse to come – for all of them.

"Well, we won't go down without a fight – that's for sure," said Roger.

"No," agreed Millicent. "We won't."

When the cell began to lighten with the sunrise, Roger stirred.

"It's time," he said.

Briar had just opened her eyes. She'd been dreaming about her mother and father. They were all travelling together in an old-fashioned, open-top car on a quiet country road in France. They stopped to look at fields of poppies and bought cheese and bread from a roadside stall. They threw off their clothes and swam in an icy river flowing down from the mountains. Then they lay on a flat rock warmed by the sun and drifted off to sleep, listening to the sound of water running over the rocks and a gentle breeze rustling through the poplar trees.

When Briar awoke, she was, of course, not on warm rock but cold concrete. As her eyes focused, she saw grey concrete blocks instead of a sparkling river. She felt numb, and then unbearably sad. Tears welled up, stinging her eyes. She tried to blink them away, but more came in a flood.

Because of the tears, she didn't notice at first that the block was moving. In fact, she heard it before she saw it – a deep grating sound. She blinked and sat up, then moved over to the wall and placed her cheek on it, looking down. One of the blocks was sticking out further than the others! As she watched, she heard a giggle and a muffled thump. She felt the gentle vibration on her cheek, and the block inched out further. Roger and Millicent were through! It had worked!

Briar dropped to her knees. As soon as the block was far enough out, she grabbed it and pulled. As more of it came through, she was able to move it faster, and before long she was grabbing it with both hands and quietly lowering it to the floor.

She leaned down and looked through the hole in the wall. There were Roger and Millicent, jostling each other for position, both trying to get a look at Briar!

"Hello, sweetheart," said Millicent, putting her hand through the wall to touch Briar's cheek. "Oh, what gorgeous red hair you have!"

"Hello, dear," said Roger, grinning broadly.

Briar couldn't help it. Seeing their lovely kind faces was too much, and she burst into tears again. For so long she had been deprived of any kindness. Now, being touched and cared for, knowing that someone worried about what happened to her, her heart welled with a long-forgotten joy.

CHAPTER 15

Flynn and Paddy barely had the strength to stagger up the beach and collapse in the dunes. It was lucky that it was a warm night, as both boys were chilled to the core from their hours in the sea. They clung together to keep warm and fell into a fitful, restless sleep.

When Paddy awoke, the first thing he saw was Lightning. The falcon sat motionless, just inches from his face, regarding him with a suspicious eye. This boy wasn't about to disappear again, was he?

Paddy rolled over and shook Flynn.

"What! Who is it?" Flynn yelled, sitting bolt upright. There was sand all over his face and several long strands of seaweed clung to his hair. He looked like some sort of sea monster.

Paddy laughed. "You'll have to get cleaned up before we head into town. You look awful."

Flynn rubbed his hands over his face. "You don't look so hot yourself."

Paddy wasn't surprised. He was still exhausted from their ordeal.

The boys stood up and brushed the debris off themselves. Their shirts and shorts were dirty and torn, and still damp. They had bruises and cuts from being caught up in the disintegrating boat and were blistered from the salt water and sunburn.

"We're going to make an entrance, that's for sure," said Flynn.

Lightning fluttered up to Flynn's shoulder and fell asleep; his watch duty was over for now.

The boys made their way to the top of the sand dunes. When they got there, the first thing they saw was a road – something they'd never seen before. They stood looking at it in utter astonishment. Finally, they stepped onto it, feeling the texture with their feet.

"It's like a super-long rock," said Paddy.

Then they did what any person would do. They followed it.

The road wound its way up the hillside above the beach to the top of a ridge. It was steep, and the boys were soon breathing heavily. As they crested the hill, they halted in astonishment. Paddy opened his mouth to say something, but no sound came out. He simply stood and stared.

As far as the eye could see, buildings covered the plain below. Houses were spread up and down the coast, while further inland there were clusters of factories and warehouses. In the distance, high-rise office towers marked what they figured was the city centre. It seemed incredible to the boys that people had been responsible for altering the landscape so completely.

Just then, the silence was broken by an awful noise – a growing roar, and a series of loud bangs. A car rounded a corner and came chugging up the road towards them. It was the first car the boys had ever seen – a beaten-up station wagon, with smoke pouring out of its exhaust. As it came closer, the boys could see at the wheel a young man with long hair and a beard, his elbow poking out of the rolled-down driver's window. Strapped to the roof was a long, slightly curved wooden plank with rounded ends. Three things shaped like dolphins' fins were stuck to one end.

The boys jumped back off the road in alarm. The man gave them a curious look as he cruised past, then his face brightened and he gave them a wink and smile. At the crest of the hill, his car backfired, making another loud bang.

"So… that's a car," said Paddy. "Give me Clappers any day."

"Agreed," replied Flynn.Nothing their mother and father had told them about the city could have prepared them for the assault on their senses they now experienced. As they walked, they saw new and incredible things everywhere. For a full five minutes, they watched a man watering his garden. The brothers just couldn't make sense of a limitless water supply coming from a long, narrow tube. Back home, carrying water from the stream to their house was one of their most tiresome chores!

They saw children of their own age riding bikes and scooters, and longed to try them out for themselves. One little boy was playing with a radio-controlled car on his driveway, and Paddy couldn't help himself. He walked up to him and asked if he could have a turn. The boy took one look at Paddy, with his ripped and dirty clothes, picked up his toy car and ran back into his house, crying out for his father.

Paddy and Flynn turned and ran.

They stopped to examine street lights and footpaths. They tried – without success – to figure out why anybody would want to build a fence. They marvelled at letterboxes and traffic lights, roadside drains and electric garage doors. In someone's front yard they saw a steel frame with a large, round mat at its centre, suspended from all sides by springs. They spent a long time trying to figure out what it could possibly be for. Anyone watching would have thought they were mad.

They were continually startled by passing cars and almost broke into a frightened run when they first saw a huge truck.

After two hours of walking, the boys were worn out. They hadn't eaten in a long time and had no water to drink. They sat down on the kerb for a rest.

"Where are we going to find something to eat?" said Paddy.

"I don't know," replied Flynn. "We can't buy anything. The money was with the rest of the stuff on the boat." The boys' mother had surprised them with a small roll of very old bank notes when they were packing for the journey. Now the notes were at the bottom of the sea. Clearly, food wasn't going to be as easy to come by as it was on the island.

The roar of an engine, followed by an almighty bang, echoed around the neighbourhood and the boys looked up to see the same old station wagon they'd seen earlier, coming along the street.

This time, however, it didn't drive past. The car pulled over to the side of the road and glided to a halt beside the boys, announcing its arrival with another monumental backfire.

The man leaned out of his window and nodded to them, smiling. Deep laughter lines radiated out from his twinkly eyes – it was obvious he smiled a lot. The boys liked him straightaway.

"We meet again," he said. "Wait… is that an eagle on your shoulder?"

"Hi," said Paddy.

"Hello," said Flynn. "No, it's a falcon."

"That's awesome!" said the man. "You boys heading into the city?"

"I think so," said Flynn. "We're not sure."

"Well, that's the most interesting thing I've heard all day. Want a lift?"

"What's a lift?" said Paddy.

The man looked at them curiously. "OK, now that's just become the most interesting thing I've heard all day. A lift is a ride in my car, so you don't have to walk for miles and miles. The city is a long way on foot."

"What's on foot?" said Paddy.

"Are you kidding me? You're on foot," said the man.

"We're sitting down," replied Paddy.

"We're on butt," said Flynn.

The man smiled. "Yes. I guess you are."

Paddy leapt to his feet. "We would like a lift."

"Paddy, I'm not sure if we should…" began Flynn, but Paddy was already striding to the car. He jumped up and slid one leg inside the open window.

"Whoa!" said the man. "What are you doing?"

"Getting into the car," replied Paddy. "Can you move over?"

The man laughed. "You could use one of the other three doors, you know."

"Oh. Right. Sorry." Paddy jumped down to the ground and raced around to the passenger door. As he ran out onto the road, he stepped straight into the path of an oncoming car, which swerved wildly to avoid him. The startled driver blared his horn at Paddy, who calmly flattened himself against the side of the station wagon.

"Oops," he said.

Then he grabbed the door and pulled. "It won't open!" he said.

The man leaned over and wound down the passenger side window. "You have to pull the lever under the handle to open it. Have you never been in a car before?"

Paddy opened the door, and jumped in next to the man. "Nope."

The man cocked an eyebrow, then shook his head in disbelief. He smiled. He looked at Flynn. "Are you coming too?"

Flynn hesitated. His exhausted body wanted to accept, and the man seemed friendly. But all the people he'd ever met from the mainland had been awful, cruel people. Eventually, he shrugged, walked around the car and slid in beside Paddy on the front bench seat. There was plenty of room for all three of them.

"I'm Kelly. Pleased to meet you," said the man, holding out his hand.

The boys stared at it. They had never shaken hands with anyone before – in their family everyone hugged each other. After a pause, both of them grabbed Kelly's hand at the same time and gave it a squeeze. They smiled at him.

"OK, that's the weirdest handshake ever, but I like it," said Kelly.

Kelly's car was jam-packed with a bewildering array of stuff – lumps of wax, envelopes, clay figurines, pieces of driftwood, boxes of matches, shells and even an empty bowl with a spoon sticking out of it all jostled for position. Paddy and Flynn looked at it all in astonishment.

"Sorry," said Kelly, "it's a bit of a mess."

He put the car into gear and the station wagon moved off slowly.

"If I treat her gently she might not backfire..."

BANG! The car let forth an impressively loud backfire.

"Or, then again, she might," said Kelly, and the boys laughed.

As the car gathered pace, Flynn and Paddy gripped the seat. It was unnerving seeing the endless roll of concrete disappearing under the car bonnet. But soon, the boys were whooping and laughing whenever Kelly drove the car around a corner.

Poor Lightning was highly confused.

"You guys weren't kidding. You really haven't been in a car before, have you?"

Kelly listened with growing astonishment as the boys told him their story. He kept shaking his head, and exclaiming "No way!" or "You've got to be kidding me." When they finally told him The Pitbull had probably kidnapped their grandparents, Kelly banged his palm on the steering wheel and whistled.

"Just tell me what you need me to do," he said.

"Take us to the police station," replied Flynn.

"No problem," said Kelly. "Fifteen minutes away, tops."

"I don't mean to be rude, Kelly," said Flynn, "but do you have any food? We haven't eaten for ages."

Kelly hit his head with his hand.

"What an idiot I am! Of course – you're starving. No problem."

He pulled over to a corner store, ran inside and emerged clutching armfuls of food and drink. The boys had never seen anything like it. Everything was wrapped in plastic or in a jar with a shiny label – aside from a bunch of bananas. Immediately, they both peeled one and gulped it down.

Kelly watched in amusement. He opened a big crackly bag. "Have you ever eaten crisps?"

The boys shook their heads and tried one each, but wrinkled their noses in disgust.

"No? Try this then," said Kelly, and he spread something brown and sticky generously between two slices of bread. Both boys took a small bite and then rapidly wolfed down the rest, smiling at each other in delight.

"This brown stuff looks terrible, but tastes amazing!" said Paddy. "What is it?"

"Peanut butter," said Kelly. "It's just mashed peanuts, I think. It goes awesome with just about anything."

If the boys enjoyed the peanut butter sandwiches, that was nothing compared to the taste sensation of eating chocolate and drinking lemonade. It was more sugar all at once than they'd ever had before. It was first time either of them had tried a fizzy drink, and they laughed at the bubbles going up their noses and the burps that followed.

Lightning, however, turned his nose up at everything they offered him.

Over lunch, Kelly told them about himself. He was twenty-three years old, and was an artist

– a painter. He didn't have much money, but he enjoyed what he did and it meant he could go surfing at the coast, something he loved to do more than anything. He took the surfboard off the roof of the car and gave them a good look at it.

The boys listened with interest, thinking of the huge waves that broke on the outer reefs of their island.

Kelly lived in the city, but wanted to move away as soon as he could. He dreamed of owning a little house on the beach somewhere, where he could paint and surf for the rest of his life, and raise a family.

After lunch, Kelly put the old car in gear again and they set off. Paddy watched and listened as Kelly showed him how to operate the car using the accelerator, clutch and brake, and making sure it was in the right gear.

"It takes a bit of practice," said Kelly. "People usually have lessons for months before they attempt their driving test."

"I reckon I could do it," said Paddy. "Can I have a go?"

Kelly laughed. "No way. I quite like living."

He manoeuvred the car into a parking space. "Look. There it is – the police station. Across the street and four doors down. Want me to go in with you?"

"We'll be fine – thanks," said Flynn.

"Well, I guess this is goodbye," said Kelly. "If you need me – for anything – call this number." He scrawled down some digits on the back of an old envelope. "Be careful. And please – look both ways before you cross the road!"

"Thanks for everything, Kelly," chorused the boys, and they did their weird three-way handshake grab again.

Paddy and Flynn stood on the curb watching Kelly chug off down the road. Just before he turned the corner at the far end of the street, the station wagon performed another almighty backfire, which reverberated around the quiet street. The boys burst out laughing.

It was then that the brothers saw something truly alarming.

The doors of a dark grey van, parked fifty yards from the police station, suddenly flew open and three men tumbled out, each holding a pistol. They'd heard the backfire and must have thought it was a gunshot.

The brothers dived behind a parked car, their hearts suddenly pounding in their chests. Lying on their bellies, they could see under the car. The men had quickly concealed their weapons, but were still looking up and down the street, searching for the source of the shot. Flynn saw one of them look across to a line of parked cars and make a hand signal.

He realised with a jolt he was looking at The Pitbull's men. Even worse, there must be more of them, sitting in a car just a few parking spaces away from where the brothers were lying!

They were waiting for Flynn and Paddy!

Flynn flattened himself to the ground.

He whispered to Paddy, and pointed. They looked down the line of cars, trying to figure out which one the second lot of men might be in. It didn't take long to find out. As they watched, a car door swung open and a thick-set man stepped out. He was just twenty feet away, dressed all in black, and holding a gun.

He looked straight at the boys and began striding towards them, his gun raised!

CHAPTER 16

N ow that Briar could talk to Millicent and Roger whenever she wanted, the discomfort of the cell was far more bearable. Through the hole in the wall, they kept up a constant conversation. Briar told Millicent and Roger all about the customs and culture of the countries she had travelled to, while they told Briar stories of the island. It sounded like a truly magical place, raw and untamed and wildly beautiful.

These conversations took place while Briar and Roger prised out the mortar from the blocks surrounding the one they'd already dislodged. They were working on an escape plan. Roger had removed the tiny prong from his belt, which doubled the speed at which they could work. It was also much easier now that one block had already been removed.

Finally, they had removed four blocks, enough to put the plan into action. They decided to try it that afternoon, when the guard came to give them their lunch.

Millicent looked at Briar through the hole in the wall. Her expression was stern, like she was about to say something very important.

"Briar, I want you to be totally honest. Are you sure you want to do this? It's likely to be dangerous. I don't know what they'll do to us if it doesn't work."

Briar smiled. "I've never been more sure of anything in my life."

CHAPTER 17

The last thing the man walking towards Flynn and Paddy expected was to be attacked from above. He was smiling, thinking to himself how easy it was going to be to capture the brothers. Then, suddenly, he couldn't see a thing. His head was buffeted and struck, and punctured in half a dozen places by something sharp. It was only when Lightning let forth a "*squee*" that the man realised it was bird! In a fury, he reached above his head, but his flailing hands grasped nothing but thin air.

The bird had disappeared. He suddenly realised he could see again, but when he looked over to where the boys had been lying, they were gone!

Flynn and Paddy were running hard along the street, away from the police station. They didn't look back, but could hear the shouts of the men, who were giving chase.

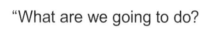

"What are we going to do? Where should we go?" panted Paddy.

"I don't know! We need to get out of the open," replied Flynn. His eyes scanned the buildings along the street. "There!"

He pointed to a small alleyway between two buildings.

As they raced towards it, Paddy chanced a look behind him – they had a sixty-yard head start on the men. If they could just get into the alley, which was too narrow for a car, they should be able to outrun them.

The alley was filthy, filled with rubbish bins and skips. It smelled of rotten food. As they ran into it, the boys startled a stray cat, which gave a yowl and tore behind a stack of old tyres.

"Flynn!" hissed Paddy, his voice thick with fear. He pointed to the far end of the alley, where a chain-link fence blocked the exit. It was at least ten feet high and along the top was a vicious tangle of barbed wire.

"Oh, no!" cried Flynn. He looked around him. A small set of stairs led up to a door in the wall – perhaps it was an opening into the rear of a store. He raced to it and tried the handle.

"It's locked," he yelled to Paddy.

"Look," said Paddy. "Can we get up there?"

He was pointing to a spot high on the side of the building, where an iron ladder was bolted to the wall. The trouble was it started twelve feet above the ground. They'd need another ladder to even make it to the bottom rung.

"We have to try," Paddy said.

The brothers backed up to the other side of the alleyway. They had barely any run-up. Flynn kicked away some bins to make more room.

He ran – there was space for only four strides. With the momentum he gathered, he ran up the vertical brick wall. He stretched out his hand… and missed the bottom rung of the ladder by six inches!

"TRY AGAIN!" screamed Paddy. They could hear the men's footsteps. He threw a heavy sack of rubbish on the ground close to the wall for Flynn to launch from.

Flynn breathed deeply, gathering his strength. He was suddenly full of anger. It wasn't going to end in this grubby alleyway – not like this. With a roar, he flew at the wall. Planting his foot on the rubbish bag, he sprang like an Olympic high jumper. He ran up the wall, eight feet, ten feet, then swivelled his body to reach for the ladder. He wouldn't get another chance. At full stretch, Flynn caught hold of the rung with one hand! His body swung out wildly, but he managed to hold on.

He scrambled up the ladder, threaded his legs through the rungs, then hung upside down, his arms outstretched. Out of the corner of his eye he saw the men enter the alleyway.

"Go!" he shouted to Paddy, while he readied himself to catch his brother.

It was Paddy's turn. He took off, planting his foot on the rubbish bag and running up the wall. He flung his hands upward, hoping his brother would catch one of them. Flynn braced his legs against the ladder and stretched as far as he could. He managed to grasp his brother's wrist, and Paddy swung up onto the ladder like a monkey into a tree.

They scrambled up the rungs, terrified. They waited for the gunshots. But, they didn't come – The Pitbull must have ordered the men to capture the brothers alive.

Instead, the men rolled one of the large skip bins underneath the ladder. One by one, they leapt up onto it and pulled themselves up the ladder. It was all done in an instant – they were fit and well trained.

Flynn and Paddy flew up the ladder, hand over hand, until they reached the roof – some five stories up. They turned and looked down. The men were coming up fast!

The brothers scanned the rooftops. A row of identical buildings stretched away down the street, each separated by similar narrow alleyways. On top of each roof was a small room, each with a doorway – probably the access door to the buildings' internal stairways. Paddy ran to the one on their rooftop and tried the handle. It was locked.

"Come on!" yelled Flynn, racing for the edge of the roof. He looked across to the next building.

There was a gap of ten feet. Then he looked down at the five storey drop.

It was a distance either of them could easily jump – on solid ground.

"You OK with this?" asked Flynn, swallowing hard.

Paddy nodded. "Easy," he said, but his voice was unsteady.

They gave themselves a run-up, then sprinted hard for the edge. Yelling in fear, they launched themselves across the gap. It felt as if they were hanging above the alleyway for an awfully long time.

Both made it, rolling on the other side before bounding to their feet. Already the men had emerged onto the rooftop behind them and were running for the gap.

The boys tried the access door: locked.

They ran for the edge of the building and leapt across the next gap without even stopping. It was only slightly less frightening than the first time. Turning, they saw that the men had all made it across the first jump. Paddy raced for the door and wrenched on the handle: locked.

Again, the mad dash for the edge. Again, the sickening leap across the five-storey canyon. Again, the door: locked.

The boys turned to run for the edge, but something about this gap looked different. As they got closer, they were dismayed to discover it was twice as wide, and completely impossible to jump across! They peered over the side of the building, but there was no ladder, either.

"This way!," shouted Flynn. He raced to the front of the building, the side that faced the street, and looked over the edge. Beneath them, under the slight overhang of the roof, was a row of windows with a six-inch-wide window ledge outside.

"Can we make it onto that ledge?" asked Paddy. It was about eight feet below them.

"If we slide over backwards on our stomachs, then lower ourselves down and hang off the edge we should be able to swing in a bit, then let go and land on the window ledge," said Flynn. He was feeling reckless – there was no way he was giving up now.

He lay down and backed over the edge. As soon as he was able, he lowered himself and hung from his fingertips. He looked down, and immediately wished he hadn't. He began to swing backwards and forwards, in and out from the wall. Taking a deep breath, Flynn let go and landed like a cat on the windowsill.

It was Paddy's turn. He threw his legs out over the ledge and worked his way off the roof. Because he was shorter than Flynn, the window ledge was even further away from his dangling feet. Beneath him was eighty feet of empty space. He started to swing, but Flynn could see that he couldn't bring himself to let go.

"Paddy," he said, hoping the calmness in his voice would help his brother to focus. "You need to do this. Let go."

Paddy took a deep breath, swung hard, and let go.

His feet struck the ledge… he wobbled, windmilling his arms furiously as he struggling to gain his balance. Finally, thankfully, he steadied. He'd made it!

Above, the boys heard an angry shout, and five heads appeared over the edge of the roof. Although the men couldn't possibly reach them, the boys shrank back on the ledge.

"YOU RATS! Don't move a muscle!" yelled one. It was the man they'd seen on the street. They could see spots of blood on his forehead from where Lightning had pecked him. His face was twisted into a furious snarl.

The man's head disappeared, only to be replaced by his feet and legs as he backed himself off the edge. He was going to jump down onto the ledge with them!

Flynn looked around in desperation. There was only one option. He didn't hesitate. He took off his shirt and wrapped it tightly around his fist.

"What are you – " began Paddy.

But his voice was drowned out by the sound of glass smashing. Flynn had driven his hand through the window! Shards of glass fell out, turning and glinting in the sunlight before shattering on the pavement far below.

In seconds, Flynn had knocked out the remaining glass from the window. It was clear enough to pass through safely. The boys leapt in, careful not to stand on the broken glass with their bare feet, and found themselves in the bedroom of a luxurious apartment.

There was no time to lose – the man had landed on the window ledge right behind them! He shouted to the men on the rooftop to go back down the ladder, surround the building, and cut off the boys' escape.

The brothers turned and raced from the bedroom, Flynn slamming the door behind them. They were in a wide corridor, furnished with a heavy armchair, a semi-circular hall table, and a mirror. They pushed the armchair and table up against the bedroom door just as the man crashed against it, then sprinted down the corridor and into a huge dining room. Despite their hurry, they couldn't help but notice the enormous chandelier hanging from the ceiling, the shag-pile rugs, and white suede furniture. It was as far from homely as they could possibly imagine.

The boys ran through an archway and found themselves in the kitchen. And there, at the end of a long marble bench, sat the owner of the apartment. He was dressed in a white bathrobe with matching slippers and was sipping delicately from a tiny cup and reading the newspaper.

"Who are you? Help! HELP!" the man screamed.

"Sorry about the window!" shouted Flynn, as they ran through the kitchen and into another hallway. Thankfully, at the end of it was the front door of the apartment.

The brothers burst through it and found themselves in a small lobby with two doors leading from it. One was a normal wooden door and the other was a stainless steel double door with an array of lights and buttons on a panel to one side.

There was a ding, and the double doors slid open. The boys were astonished. It appeared to be nothing more than a tiny steel room! They were even more amazed to see a woman step out. She was dressed all in white and carried a white leather handbag. Her nails were long and painted white and her hair was white blonde. Flynn couldn't help but think of the White Witch in the children's book *The Lion, The Witch and The Wardrobe*. She looked at them in shock and distaste. The boys figured she must be married to the man in the robe.

"Good morning," they said politely.

Flynn and Paddy had no intention of getting into the small steel box. They wrenched open the wooden door and were relieved to see it was a stairwell. Taking the stairs three at a time, they reached the ground floor in thirty seconds. Crashing sounds above let them know that the man had busted out of the apartment and was in hot pursuit.

The boys burst back out onto the street and ran towards the police station, hoping they could reach it before the men did. Above them, Paddy heard a "*squee*" from Lightning. It was a warning that the man had emerged from the building behind them and was chasing them along the street.

Finally, they came in sight of the police station. Their breath came in ragged gasps, and their hearts pounded from the exertion.

They stopped in horror. At the foot of the steps to the station stood one of the men. He must have stayed behind in case the brothers doubled back! He noticed them immediately and began to jog towards them.

"What now?" cried Flynn.

It was at that moment that Flynn noticed they were just a few yards from the men's grey van. A mad thought sprung to his mind.

"Paddy – look! The van!"

Paddy understood immediately. He didn't hesitate.

"I'll drive!" he yelled.

He ran to the driver's door and flung it open. There, hanging in the ignition, were the keys.

"Want a lift?" he said to Flynn.

"Oh boy…" said Flynn, but a broad grin spread across his face.

"Hey, what are you doing? Get away from that van!" shouted the man who had been guarding the police station. He was now coming towards them at a full sprint.

Flynn opened the passenger door and leapt in. He wound down the window and whistled. Lightning immediately swooped in and landed on the seat between the boys. Paddy turned the key and the engine coughed once, then roared into life. He stood on the accelerator and the engine screamed.

"It's not moving!" he yelled.

"Don't you have to put it into gear?" yelled
Flynn. He was nervously watching the man on the
pavement, now no more than fifteen yards away.

Paddy hauled on the gearstick and stomped on
the accelerator again. The van bucked and vibrated,
but refused to budge. The man was almost at the
window. In the wing mirror, Paddy could see that the
other men from the rooftop were now almost upon
them too!

Flynn looked desperately at the controls. He
pulled a lever and the wipers whipped back and

forth across the windscreen. Another lever started off a flashing light and a ticking sound. Then he noticed a handle with a button on the end of it. It was at an angle, jutting up between the front seats. In desperation, he grabbed it and pressed the button. He felt something release as he lowered the handle.

Suddenly the van sprang away, lurching wildly towards the car in front. The police station guard was at the window, but he backed away in alarm. Paddy swung on the steering wheel. The engine roared and the wheels spun. The van smashed into the car in front, shunting it forward. It gave them just enough room to get out. Fishtailing wildly, the van squealed out onto the street. It swerved one way and then the next, before Paddy finally brought it under control, narrowly missing a passing delivery truck.

"Yaahoo!" whooped Paddy. "If only Kelly could see me now!"

CHAPTER 18

When the lift opened and the cook walked out, pushing the lunch trolley, the guard glared at him. He had interrupted a good video game. The guard wasn't supposed to have a phone, but he was stuck with the world's most boring job – keeping a watch on prisoners in a prison that was impossible to break out of. He needed something to do all day.

"Leave it here," he ordered.

When the cook left, the guard took a look under the dish covers. Under each was a slice of buttered bread, a dry chunk of cheese, and an apple. He ate one of the slices of bread and an apple, before rising from his seat. His bones ached from sitting in the chair for so long – his shift had begun at five o'clock that morning. Wearily, he wheeled the trolley down the corridor.

It took him a long time to find the key for Briar's cell in the bunch hanging from his belt. No doubt the girl inside could hear them jangling. She'd be starving – her last meal was the previous afternoon, and he'd eaten most of it himself. Serves her right, he thought to himself.

He put the key into the lock and turned it. Roughly, he kicked the door and it swung back, banging against the wall.

"Lunch…" he began, but fell silent. His jaw dropped. He gaped. His eyes boggled. Frantically, he scanned the cell. She was gone!

Stupidly, he ran inside and checked every corner. He even looked into the toilet. A prickling fear rose in his throat – his life wouldn't be worth living if she had escaped on his watch.

Sprinting back into the corridor, the guard fell over the lunch trolley and went sprawling on the floor. A searing pain ran up his leg. Looking down, he saw blood from a cut on his knee beginning to soak through his trousers.

He scrambled to his feet and raced back along the corridor. Then, halfway along, he was brought skidding to a stop by an awful thought. What if…

He sprinted back to the cell door of the old couple – Millicent and what's-his-name. Fumbling for the key, he dropped the bunch on the floor and cursed loudly. His hands were shaking. Finally he found it and turned it in the door.

He was afraid to look. Slowly, he pushed open the heavy steel door and walked inside. There, in the far corner of the cell, was Briar!

"Hello!" she said brightly. "Is it lunch time already?"

The guard simply stood and stared.

"How…" he began, but then he heard a tiny sound behind him. The rest of his sentence was lost when, from behind the door, Millicent sprang, grabbing his ankle. The old man shoved him in the back. The guard bellowed as he fell, but the air was knocked out of him when Briar, Roger and Millicent all leapt on his back. They pulled his hands up behind him and he felt them being lashed together.

Then, the three prisoners leapt off and ran to the door. He screamed at them and tried to get to his feet, but without the use of his arms he slipped and fell again, striking his head hard against the concrete floor. His vision clouded. The last thing he heard before he passed out was the key turning in the cell door.

CHAPTER 19

"Go easy," hissed Flynn. "There could be a trap."

The boys were taking no chances. They wriggled under the hedge at the back of the property and kept low as they ran across the lawn and crouched down behind a row of runner beans trailing their way up a wire frame. Of course, Paddy snapped one off and ate it.

They watched the house for a long time, before figuring it was safe to approach. Running quickly around to the side, they stood under the window, listening hard. There wasn't a sound. Slowly, carefully, the boys poked their heads up and looked in the window of their grandparents' home.

Not knowing what else to do, the brothers had decided to head for their grandparents' house. Although they knew the address by heart, they didn't have a clue how to find it.

It hadn't been easy, driving around a big city with an eleven-year-old at the wheel. Paddy had wrestled with the van as it jerked, skidded and swerved. It seemed to have a mind of its own. The tyres squealed and smoked when he was too enthusiastic with the accelerator, and bunny-hopped and stalled when he didn't push it down enough.

On a quiet street, the boys had pulled over to ask directions from a man walking along the footpath. He was dressed most oddly. His jacket matched his trousers, and he had a colourful piece of material tied around his neck.

When Paddy leaned out of the window to ask him how to get to Brookvale – the suburb where their grandparents lived – he didn't answer.

His mouth had set in a grim line and he'd pulled out his phone and punched in some numbers.

"I want the police, please," the boys heard him say. "You need to get here quickly. There's a child driving a van..."

Flynn had looked at Paddy. "Best we keep moving."

Paddy had stamped on the accelerator and the engine roared. The man was showered with dust and gravel as the van, tires spinning, raced away.

After that, the boys had been more careful. Paddy had parked the van down the street while Flynn walked into a shop to ask for directions. Slowly, after many wrong turns and near misses, they'd parked the van a block away from their grandparents' house, deciding to walk the rest of the way. Instead of using the footpath, they'd crept through people's backyards, staying out of sight in case any more of

The Pitbull's men were watching the house. They'd sent Lightning up on lookout, but no sound came from the sharp-eyed falcon.

All was quiet. No cars were parked on the street out front and no one was on the footpath.

But now the boys regretted having come. What they saw through the window chilled them to the core. Tables and chairs had been turned upside down; shelves had been tipped onto the floor and paintings ripped from the walls. Shattered glass and crockery were spread across the kitchen floor. A door hung from one hinge.

There was no one inside, and not a sound to be heard.

They crept around to the back door of the house. It was wide open. Where the lock should have been was just a mess of splintered wood – The Pitbull's men must have kicked it in. The boys entered, walking carefully through the wreckage of their grandparents' lives. They split up and walked from room to room in silence, imagining the fear their grandparents must have felt at this terrible invasion.

On the bedroom floor, Flynn found a framed photo of their whole family standing on the beach on the island. He figured it was taken about four years ago – Ada was just a baby. It made him unbearably sad. And angry. A tear ran down his cheek.

Suddenly, Paddy gave a shout from the kitchen. Flynn's heart leapt into his mouth, and he dropped the frame and ran. He skidded into the kitchen. A piece of broken glass jabbed into his heel, but he didn't care.

Paddy was standing motionless, staring at a black box on the kitchen table – the one piece of furniture in the house that remained upright. A blue light winked at the boys. A faint hum came from it. Beside it lay a mobile phone.

"What do you think it is?" asked Flynn.

Before Paddy could answer, it crackled into life, whirring and humming before spitting out a piece of paper onto the table.

The boys stared at it. The page was covered in random letters which made no sense. In its centre was the dog's head – The Pitbull's insignia. It was obviously a code.

They had seen The Pitbull's coded messages before. They knew what to do.

Paddy snatched up the phone from beside the printer, pushing the button at the bottom to start it up. There, in the centre of the screen, was the square icon with the letters 'AR' on it. Paddy tapped it and held it over the page.

a P t   o   l

s u w i g e a   l l   .

e f u f a l t l s n i t

n l a a t i b w i a i e

y e I p e g h r t   s

e n o v e u y o r   e

r e w g i p i n i n t p

o c n t e m u d I d s r

h , r . T t a   u u

u   s o

Use the **AR Reads** app on your device to crack this code.

Simply start up the app, then point the device at this page and check out the message from The Pitbull. If you don't have a device – don't worry – just read on!

As they watched, the letters arranged themselves into a message, which couldn't have been clearer. A car was going to pull up outside and they needed to get into it or say goodbye to their grandparents forever. It sent a shiver down their spines.

Paddy put the phone into his pocket and picked up the sheet of paper. If they ever made it to the police, he would show it to them as evidence. But to his amazement, the code on the page was fading before his eyes. The ink got lighter and lighter, until it couldn't be seen at all. The printer on the table then made a loud electric zap, and a cloud of smoke puffed out of it. The Pitbull was covering his tracks!

From outside came the sound of an engine and through the window they saw a long black car pull into the driveway. The back door swung open, but no one got out. The car waited there, its engine running. The windows were tinted, so they couldn't see the driver.

"We don't have a choice, do we?" said Paddy.

Flynn shook his head. "No. We don't."

The brothers suddenly felt exhausted. After all they'd been through, they were now left with no other option than to deliver themselves to The Pitbull.

They left the house and walked towards the waiting car. Peering inside, they saw that the back seat was empty. Reluctantly, they climbed in.

A black glass window separated the front and back seats. They couldn't speak to or even see the driver. The doors closed automatically and the brothers heard the locking mechanism click. Flynn immediately tried the handle – it was locked. It was too late to change their minds. They were trapped.

"Are you sure this is the right thing to do?" said Paddy. He kicked the seat in front of him angrily. "I reckon we could smash the glass and jump out of the window right now."

Flynn held his head in his hands. "I don't know."

"This might be a trick," said Paddy.

"Our grandparents could have escaped from the men and be hiding somewhere! Maybe The Pitbull's men just took her ring from the house and sent it to lure us away from the island."

"I've thought of that," replied Flynn, "but we have no way of knowing – and if we're wrong…" His voice trailed off. It was too awful to say the words out loud.

The boys sat in silence as the car travelled through the streets towards the centre of the city. The buildings here were higher and closer together. It was like being in a canyon, except this one had been made by people.

The car turned into a long, narrow street. A forty-storey skyscraper stood at the far end. Near its top they could see the dog's head on a large billboard.

Paddy jumped: something was vibrating in his pocket. It was the phone he had taken from his grandparents' home. He pulled it out, and setting his jaw, tapped on the green button to answer it.

CHAPTER 20

Briar, Millicent and Roger had made it no further than the end of the corridor. To summon the lift, they needed a code for the electronic keypad. Briar spent half an hour tapping in random numbers, but it was hopeless. All three, meanwhile, were doing their best to stay out of sight of the security cameras, positioned all around the lift.

Without warning, the lift pinged and the doors began to open! Through the widening crack they saw a figure.

Someone was coming! And there was nowhere to hide.

Realising their escape plan had failed, Roger stepped out to confront whoever was coming. To his surprise, he came face to face with the cook, who had returned to collect the lunch trolley.

"Hey! What are you doing out here?" said the cook. His face was a mask of fear and confusion.

Briar and Millicent stepped out from behind Roger. They smiled at the cook.

"We're leaving," said Millicent. "And you're going to help us."

The cook yelped, turned, and ran back into the lift. But before the doors could close, Roger, Millicent and Briar had joined him.

"Ground floor, please," said Briar.

CHAPTER 21

The brothers sat in the back of the car, listening grimly to The Pitbull's voice. He had called them on the phone Paddy had taken from their grandparents' house, and it was obvious he was enjoying himself immensely.

Use the **AR Reads** app on your device to hear The Pitbull's chilling phone conversation.

Simply start up the app, then point the device at this page and check out the message from The Pitbull. If you don't have a device – don't worry – just read on!

When Paddy answered the phone, he'd suspected the voice he'd hear would be The Pitbull's. And he knew The Pitbull would warn them not to attempt to escape. Both proved to be true.

Yet Paddy and Flynn had been planning exactly that. Flynn was lying down across the seat on his back, his feet in the air. He was preparing to kick out the window.

But when the brothers heard their grandmother's panic-stricken voice over the phone, they hesitated. This was proof that The Pitbull was holding their grandparents as prisoners. Their hearts sank. Flynn lowered his feet.

Their grandmother pleaded with them over the phone to stay away. But The Pitbull quickly cut her off, and Paddy and Flynn knew they couldn't abandon their grandparents. Besides, it was already too late. The car had turned into the skyscraper's vehicle entrance and was pulling up outside the huge glass doors of the lobby. A dozen of The Pitbull's men quickly surrounded them, their guns at the ready.

Paddy and Flynn climbed out and were marched into the lobby. There, standing in a forlorn group of three, were their grandparents and a girl of about their own age. Flynn suddenly had a jolt of recognition – she was the girl who'd been on the deck of The Pitbull's ship – the girl who had freed the dragons!

Millicent cried out when she saw her grandsons. The boys knew they must look truly wretched. Their clothes were torn, their faces were dirty, and they were covered in bruises and cuts.

"Oh no," said Roger.

"Hi Grandad. Hi Grandma," said Paddy. He gave a weak smile.

Flynn looked at them grimly. He was struggling to control his anger.

The Pitbull clapped his hands together in delight.

"Well. Isn't this touching? A family reunion. How wonderful!"

Then his face soured.

"Why don't you go back upstairs. You can catch up there – I assure you there will be plenty of time. I've arranged a special dinner for you all, to be served in your cells. Horse meat stew."

He laughed as his captives were taken away.

The Pitbull beckoned to the cook. The poor man hesitated, but was shunted forward by one of the guards. He stood before his boss, his knees shaking wildly.

The Pitbull leaned forward, bringing his face inches from the cook's.

"You were helping them to escape?"

"N-n-no, sir," he stammered. "They forced me…"

"Forced by two geriatrics and a little girl, were you?" the Pitbull cut in. Without warning, he viciously clouted the man across the head. The cook went sprawling on the ground and The Pitbull stood over him.

"Take him away," he ordered. "Lock him up with that pathetic excuse for a guard upstairs. I never want to see either of them again."

When the cook's screaming finally faded away down the corridor, The Pitbull allowed himself a moment of self-congratulations. He had done it! Now, nothing stood in his way. He was free to fulfil his dream of capturing the island's dragons and bringing them back here to create the world's greatest zoo exhibit! Those pathetic brothers could do nothing to stop him.

He had so much to do! There was no time to lose!

The Pitbull looked around. Every last one of his men had gone. Idiots. In a rage he yelled for them, until half a dozen scrambled back into the lobby and stood waiting for orders.

The Pitbull barked out his instructions. "Prepare the ship. I want it ready to leave for the island in two days. And begin work on the dragon enclosure."

CHAPTER 22

"**S**quee!"

Lightning flew in circles, around and around The Pitbull's tower, calling in distress.

The city was a bewildering place. The constant roar of traffic rose up from the endless roads, and horrible, toxic smoke drifted up from factories and coal-fired power stations. There was little wildlife – hardly anything to eat for a hungry falcon.

Lightning had followed the car with the brothers in it, watching closely as it sped through the streets to the city centre. Tall towers made the wind swirl and buffet, and the falcon had to continually adjust his wings to stay level.

Lightning saw the car disappear beneath a building. Confused, he swooped down. But he couldn't see Flynn and Paddy anywhere.

CHAPTER 23

The mood back in the cells was awful. All five prisoners were locked in Briar's, while the guards worked in Millicent and Roger's, welding a huge steel plate across the wall. There would be no more removing of the blocks. Once the work was complete, the prisoners would again be split up and kept apart.

Paddy paced the cell, examining every crack in the wall. Briar watched him.

"I've already done that – about a million times."

"Yeah? Well, you may have missed something."

"I don't think so," said Briar. "But you go right ahead and waste your time."

Paddy rounded on her.

"You know what? How about you just keep quiet! It's your horrible uncle who's responsible for this, and because you're related to him I'm guessing you're not too nice either!"

Briar strode over to Paddy.

"How dare you! I'm nothing like him! Take that back!"

"We don't know the first thing about you," said Paddy. "You could be a spy, keeping an eye on us for your uncle."

Millicent spoke in a gentle voice.

"Paddy, calm down. We've learned lots about Briar, and believe me, she's on our side."

"She freed the dragons on the ship, Paddy – don't forget that," added Flynn.

Paddy looked at Briar, who stared back at him, her eyes flashing.

"OK. I'm sorry," said Paddy.

Briar softened. "Me too."

They heard a scuffling sound. At the window a pigeon scrambled to its feet and flew away, as if panicked by something.

There was silence for a moment before they again heard the flutter of beating wings, accompanied by another sound: "*squee!*"

"Lightning!" chorused the brothers.

Flynn leapt to his feet and raced to the window. It was too high to reach, but Lightning hopped in through the bars and stood on the sill, sternly looking down at them all. He seemed deeply unimpressed that they had allowed themselves to be captured and imprisoned high in a tower in the middle of a noisy, smelly city.

The boys tried time and time again to entice Lightning to fly down to them, but he wouldn't budge. Finally, sometime in the middle of the afternoon, he gave a pitiful cry then hopped out through the bars of the window.

Lightning spread his wings and flew away.

Tears ran down the boys' faces. They sensed that the falcon had said goodbye.

Millicent and Roger could do little to console the boys, and Briar looked like she might cry too.

"This is all our fault," said Flynn. "Paddy and I messed it all up."

"Nonsense," replied Millicent, hugging her grandsons. "If anyone is to blame, it's Roger and me, for allowing ourselves to be caught."

Briar stood up and looked at them all. Her voice wavered with emotion.

"That's quite enough – all of you. No one is to blame except my uncle."

They lapsed into silence, each lost in their thoughts. The small circle of sunlight coming through the window slowly rose up the opposite wall as the sun set. Exhausted, hungry and utterly depressed, one by one they slipped into a troubled sleep.

CHAPTER 24

"**P**addy! Wake up!"

Paddy sat bolt upright in the cell.

It took him a few moments to realise where he was, and that his brother had woken him.

"You were calling out in your sleep," whispered Flynn.

Paddy rubbed his eyes and looked at Flynn. His brother looked awful – wide-eyed yet exhausted.

"Sorry," said Paddy. "Did I wake you?"

Flynn shook his head. "I haven't slept all night."

Flynn and Paddy lay down again, but sleep

wouldn't come. Terrible thoughts cycled relentlessly through their minds. How would they ever get out? What would happen when their parents came looking for them? Would they ever see their island again? The answers were too awful to consider.

"*Squee!*"

Lightning! The brothers almost leapt out of their skins at the sound of their falcon. It was still quite dark, although in the east the sky had begun to lighten, so they could just make out the bird's silhouette.

"He didn't leave us after all," said Paddy.

"Lightning," whispered Flynn. "Here boy…"

This time Lightning didn't stay on the sill, but rather fluttered down silently into the cell, landing on the floor between the boys. They stroked him gently. Seeing the bird lifted their spirits greatly.

Briar was awoken by the sound of the boys' excited voices, and she lay on her side, propped up on her elbow, smiling at them.

"He came back," she said.

Then, in the silence, the three children heard an unusual sound. It was coming from the cell window. It sounded like the beating wings of a pigeon, but with a slower, deeper rhythm. It was getting louder. Whatever it was, it was coming closer.

"CLANG!"

Something hit the bars of the high window with tremendous force and the whole room shook with the impact.

The children flattened themselves on the floor and scrambled to the far side of the room. Roger and Millicent woke in fright, and Roger let out a confused shout.

"Earthquake!"

But it wasn't an earthquake. When the prisoners looked up at the window, what they saw made them gasp in disbelief. Wrapped around the iron bars were the huge talons of a dragon!

"Elton!" the brothers cried out together, leaping for joy. They could scarcely believe it. Paddy was so excited he ran at the wall, leapt high and managed to grasp the windowsill. He pulled himself up and found himself face to face with their beautiful dragon.

"Oh, Elton! Are we glad to see you! Lightning came to get you, didn't he? You clever bird, Lightning!"

Flynn stood motionless in the cell. He looked dumbfounded.

Their brave and clever falcon had spent half the night flying to the island to find Elton, then somehow managed to get the dragon to follow him back to the mainland! Now, the boys fully realised the extent of the understanding between the bird and the dragons – it seemed they could communicate on a very deep level indeed.

From the window ledge, Paddy gave a shout of surprise.

"Iris is here, too! She just flew past!"

Flynn punched the air, but their joy was short-lived. From outside in the corridor came the sound of running footsteps. Before any of them could react, the door swung open and two guards came rushing in.

"What's going on in here?" yelled one of them. "What was that noise?" In his hands he held an ugly, snub-nosed gun.

"Earthquake," piped up Roger. "I hope this building is well built."

Miraculously, Elton was quiet, hanging on to the bars of the window. Paddy guessed he was taking a much-needed rest after such a long flight.

The guards looked nervously at the walls and ceiling, as if they were about to fall in at any moment. In the darkness, neither of them noticed Elton's talons, still locked around the bars.

"And who's Elton?" asked the second guard. "I heard one of you shouting his name."

As if to answer the question, Elton chose that moment to wrench on the bars of the window. They made an awful metallic screech as he ripped them clean out of the wall and dropped them down the side of the building. They tumbled through the still night air and clanged to the ground far below.

Then, Elton decided to properly introduce himself. He forced his snout into the window opening and shot a vicious fireball straight at the two guards! Millicent and Roger were closest to them, and had to turn their faces away from the intense heat.

The guards turned and ran, slapping furiously at their scorched clothing.

As the guards retreated down the corridor, Briar noticed they had left their keys in the lock. She pulled them out, slammed the cell door and locked it from the inside.

"That should give us a little more time," she said with a grin.

"Nicely done." Paddy and Briar high-fived.

"That's all very well, but what do we do now?" said Roger.

Again, Elton provided the answer. He withdrew his head and ripped furiously at the concrete wall with raking slashes of his talons. The concrete crumbled away, exposing the internal steel beams that formed the structure of the building. But even Elton was no match for these – they were simply too big. Iris arrived at his side, and together they hauled on the beams with all their incredible strength, but they simply wouldn't budge. Not even an inch.

CHAPTER 25

The Pitbull was jolted awake by a loud clang somewhere on the street below. It sounded like a blacksmith hammering on an anvil.

"What the devil…"

Cursing, he rolled out of bed and walked to the window. He pulled back the curtain and scanned the street below. His bedroom took up the entire thirtieth floor of the tower, so he was afforded a good view all around.

There was no movement at all on the street, and everything was quiet. He unlatched the window and pushed it open, breathing in the cool night air. The twinkling lights of the city spread like a glittering blanket across the land, right to the coast. Out on the harbour, he could just make out the lights of a couple of fishing trawlers. Beyond that was the deep black of the open sea. Out there, waiting for him, was an island chock-full of dragons – the key to his great fame and fortune. A smile spread across his face.

The Pitbull needed to visit the bathroom. Just as he reached out to close the window, there was the most incredible explosion of shattering glass and tearing steel. He reeled backwards into the bedroom and toppled over, stunned. Eventually, realising he was unhurt, The Pitbull staggered to his feet. Warily he approached the window again, and was amazed to see it had gone! He peered out onto the street and spotted the mangled frame far below. It had been completely ripped away by a falling slab of concrete, which now lay in broken chunks all over the street.

Then, he spotted something else. Squinting to make it out in the glare of the streetlights, he saw, lying on the footpath, the circular steel grille from one of the cells! But how…

"Sir! Sir! Wake up, sir!"

One of his men was furiously pounding on the door. Dazed, The Pitbull opened it.

"Sorry to bother you, sir, but we have a problem," said a frightened-looking guard.

CHAPTER 26

The steel beams were too strong. But Elton had one more trick.

He forced his head into the cell and roared. He roared as the brothers had never heard him roar before. The sheer volume seemed to bend the very air. Everyone in the cell clapped their hands to their ears, but it made little difference.

Over and over he roared, until it was obvious to the prisoners that they had no choice – they had to get out of the cell.

Briar turned the key and flung open the door and they stumbled out into the corridor, reeling from the shock. Flynn slammed the cell door closed again, but still they had to walk the length of the corridor before the noise became bearable.

"What is Elton doing?" cried Paddy.

Flynn shook his head. His ears were ringing.

"I don't know." He glanced towards the lift, expecting to see the guards returning, guns raised. But they were nowhere to be seen. They must have gone down in the lift.

Then, the roaring stopped. They looked back down the corridor at the cell door. There was an eerie silence.

"Do you think it's safe…" began Briar, but she trailed off.

In the gap beneath the door, they saw a bright orange glow. As they watched, it turned from deep orange, to bright yellow, then to a blinding white. A gentle hiss rose to a crackling roar. The door began to bend and warp before their eyes as it, too, changed colour, from steel grey to a fierce scarlet. Finally, it simply melted off its hinges and crashed to the ground.

Now that the door was down, they could see what was going on. Huge streams of fire from both Elton and Iris filled the cell. They could feel the incredible heat from the end of the corridor.

"They're trying to melt the beams!" cried Paddy.

They watched, transfixed by the incredible spectacle.

Millicent, who was backed up against the lift doors, shrinking away from the intense heat, suddenly gasped.

"I can feel the lift moving! Someone's coming!"

Roger leapt into action, grabbing the two guards' chairs and dragging them over to the lift.

"You lot, help me pull open the lift doors!" he yelled. "Millicent, when we get them open, push the chairs in and let's see if we can jam the lift."

They did as he said, forcing their fingertips

between the double steel doors and pulling with all their might.

The doors opened a fraction.

"That's it," cried Roger, and he jammed his foot into the door. "Take a rest, and then pull again."

The lights above the lift showed that it was on the thirtieth floor, where it seemed to have stopped.

"Now – heave!"

Flynn and Paddy each hauled on a door. The gap widened more and more, then Briar flung herself between them, her feet on one side and her back against the other. She pushed with all her strength. Together, they managed to open them halfway.

"Just throwing the chairs in won't work," puffed Briar. "They'll land on the roof of the lift but they won't stop it. Millicent, hand one of them to me."

Millicent passed a chair to Briar, who pulled it across her body and dangled it down into the lift shaft.

"Can you hold the doors open?" she asked the boys.

"Got it," said Flynn.

"Me too!" said Paddy.

"Roger, hold my legs," commanded Briar. She wriggled onto her stomach and shuffled out over the black void. Roger knelt down and held her calves. The lift was moving again. They could feel the wind rushing up the shaft it as it raced up towards them. Briar wouldn't even see it coming in the darkness.

The boys watched Briar lean down into the abyss and look around. Next to her head, a cable hissed up the wall of the shaft, hauling the lift quickly upwards. The cable was tucked inside a recess that was just big enough for the chair to fit in.

As Briar jammed it into the gap, she called, "I can't let it go – it'll fall. I'll have to wait until the lift gets here. Roger– get ready to pull me up! Millicent, you call out which floor the lift is on!"

"I'm ready," Roger replied, but his voice cracked with worry.

Millicent looked up at the lights. "Thirty seven! Thirty eight! Thirty…"

"Now!" cried Briar, and Roger pulled for all he was worth.

At the same instant, the lift crunched into the chair. A terrible crash and the shriek of twisting metal rose from the lift shaft.

Briar and Roger tumbled backwards, falling away from the lift doors, just as Flynn and Paddy let them go. The doors clanged back together.

In the silence that followed, all five held their breath, listening intently. The lights above the lift showed it had reached the thirty-ninth floor, but the doors remained closed. They heard a muffled shout. It sounded as if it was coming from inside a closet.

"That's my uncle," said Briar.

Flynn smiled. "He sounds a bit grumpy."

Then The Pitbull's voice came loud and clear from a speaker on the keypad beside the lift.

"CAN YOU HEAR ME? CAN YOU? OPEN THE DOORS RIGHT NOW, OR ELSE…"

CRUNCH! Paddy smashed the other chair into the keypad, hitting it again and again until it was nothing more than shards of broken plastic and stray wires.

He looked up at Briar and Flynn and grinned. "Do you think that's the correct code?"

"Let's go!" said Flynn, and all five turned and raced back down the corridor.

Elton and Iris had made short work of the super-heated steel. They had slashed through it with their talons and teeth, and peeled it back as easily as a person might peel a banana. Where the cell wall had once stood, there was now a gaping hole big enough to drive a car through. Small fires burned all around the edge, and exposed electrical wiring sparked and crackled.

But there was one major problem. The concrete floor and remaining steel still glowed red and was giving off so much heat that the children could go no further than the cell doorway.

Elton realised that they couldn't reach him. Folding back his wings, he used his powerful legs to drive his huge body into the cell. He tore out enough blocks around the door to get his head through, then lay down on the ground. His body now stretched right through the cell, while his tail protruded outside the building, almost six hundred feet above the street. Meanwhile, Iris rested outside, clinging to the wall like an enormous bat.

"He wants us to walk over him – to use him as a pathway!" cried Paddy, suddenly understanding. "Clever boy, Elton! You go first, Grandma."

Millicent gulped, but didn't have a choice. As she climbed onto Elton's head, he didn't flinch. She set off along his body, crawling on her hands and knees, recoiling from the intense heat coming at her from all sides. She was like a chicken roasting in an oven.

"Move faster," called Flynn. "You have to get outside."

Millicent moved as quickly as she could, but as she edged closer to Elton's tail, where his body narrowed, it was clear she was having difficulty keeping her balance. Finally, she made it, and they saw her taking deep breaths of the cool air from outside.

"I can do this," they heard her say, although she looked as if she wasn't at all sure that she could.

Iris had taken to the air and was hovering just below Elton's tail, so Millicent could drop onto her back.

Lying flat on the end of Elton's tail, Millicent swung her legs out and dangled them over the side. She slid off as far as she could. They saw her arms trembling with the strain of trying to hold onto Elton's tail.

"Don't look down," called Roger.

Her feet flailed. She was unable to drop far enough to get to Iris.

But Iris knew what to do. With a few powerful flaps of her wings, she rose upwards. Millicent's feet touched the dragon's back, and all at once she let go of Elton's tail.

Millicent landed squarely between Iris's wings, but then lost her balance. She screamed in fear. But Iris sensed her unsteadiness, and swooped upward. The sudden force made Millicent's legs collapse underneath her, and she found herself sprawled, safely, on Iris's back.

"Oh, you clever creature!" said Millicent, patting Iris's neck.

Roger had already begun his journey along Elton's body, and soon reached his tail. With Millicent's help, he was able to climb onto Iris's back easily enough, although he would later tell the boys it was the most frightening moment of his life.

As Briar was climbing onto Elton's back, there came a loud bang from behind them. It sounded like a gunshot!

Flynn sprinted back along the corridor until he could see the lift. The doors were opening! The Pitbull and his men were forcing them apart, levering them with the barrels of their guns.

"They're coming!" he yelled, racing back to the cell.

Paddy didn't hesitate. He leapt onto Elton's back with Briar, spun around and pulled back on the dragon's spines. Immediately Elton began to move, hauling his body backwards through the cell door. Briar cried out in fear.

Flynn had almost reached the cell, but behind him, The Pitbull had emerged from the lift. Glancing back over his shoulder, Flynn saw that he carried a pistol in each hand.

"Run, Flynn!" Paddy screamed.

Flynn raced into the cell and immediately felt the ferocious heat of the floor under his feet. A lifetime of walking barefoot had toughened his skin, but in spite of this, searing pain shot up through both feet. He took two more steps before leaping through the air like an Olympic long jumper.

Behind him, a shot rang out, and he felt a rush of air as the speeding bullet zipped past just inches from his ear.

Elton's entire body was now outside of the cell. He didn't spread his wings, but instead simply allowed gravity to pull him backwards out of the building.

Flynn had timed his leap to perfection. He landed on all fours, like a cat, on Elton's head. Elton reacted immediately, jerking his head upwards and flipping the boy over onto his back. It was unexpected, and Flynn cried out in fright. Paddy and Briar only just managed to grab him, stopping him from sliding off the side of the dragon.

In the same instant, Elton released his grip on the building and they fell backwards, plummeting into the darkness below.

A volley of bullets and an enraged shout flew out into the space above them. Then came an inhuman scream of pain from The Pitbull. He must have run into the cell not knowing it would be like walking on lava!

The children had just three seconds of free-fall in which to establish a good grip on Elton before he extended his wings and pulled up so hard they felt dizzy. He flapped furiously to gain altitude, rising up out of the canyon of the city's buildings, up into the fresh night air.

CHAPTER 27

I t's not a well-known fact, but dragons don't enjoy being on yachts. And after more than three hundred miles of bobbing around on Roger and Millicent's, they were making that very clear. Iris roared and clawed at the sea, while Elton was obviously feeling seasick. His great head lay flat on the deck between his forelegs. He hadn't moved all day.

Flynn and Paddy had kept them on board for fear they wouldn't be able to make it home. The dragons were clearly exhausted from the trip to the mainland. The yacht bogged and wallowed under their terrific weight, and even small waves crashed over the side, showering them all with seawater.

Flynn looked up at the sun. "How much further is it, Grandma?"

"Just under two hundred miles, I reckon," she replied.

Paddy had been dozing on the deck, but now he sat up and looked at Flynn. He knew exactly what his brother was thinking.

"Reckon they can make it?" he asked.

Flynn nodded. "They're well rested. They'll make it."

"Then what are we waiting for?" replied Paddy, a broad smile spreading across his face. He ran to Elton and leapt upon his back.

"Come on, boy!" he yelled. Elton suddenly sprang to life. He stood and shook himself all over like a dog, roaring with excitement. Paddy stroked his neck.

"Want to come too, Grandad?" Paddy asked, although he already knew the answer.

"No, thank you, Paddy," replied Roger. "They're wonderful creatures, but if I never ride a dragon again in my life, it will be too soon."

Paddy laughed, and tweaked Elton's spines. It was all the encouragement Elton needed, and he launched himself into the air. The yacht listed alarmingly over to the side where Iris remained. She looked hopefully at Flynn.

"You ready, girl?" he asked.

She sent out a billow of white smoke in reply.

"Flynn?" Briar. "Do you think she could handle two?" said Briar.

"I reckon so. Do want to fly her?"

Briar smiled. "Do I ever!"

Iris quivered with anticipation as the children climbed on her back. Already Paddy and Elton were a distant speck in the blue.

"See you soon," Millicent called.

"Bye Grandma. Bye Grandad."

"Safe sailing," said Briar.

"Give her spines a little tug – upward and forward," instructed Flynn. Briar did as she was told, and Iris bunched her legs beneath her. Then, she sprang into the air, her yellow wings brilliant in the sunlight as she rose into the sky.

CHAPTER 28

The sight of the island made the children's hearts soar. The boys saw it with fresh eyes – the grime, pollution and overcrowding of the city gave them a brand new appreciation of their home. They suddenly realised just how lucky they were to live there.

For Briar, the sight of the beautiful valleys, mountains, lakes, and rivers were like a balm for all the hurt and sadness she'd endured. Tears streamed from her eyes as she looked down upon it and thought of her parents, and how she wished they could be with her to visit this place.

"There's our home!" Flynn pointed down at a magnificent lagoon and Briar could just make out a little wooden cottage in the trees.

"Push her spines down a bit and she'll start to descend," said Flynn.

Briar eased Iris's spines downward, but the dragon didn't respond. She pushed them down a little more, but still Iris kept on her path. Already they had passed over the house and were heading towards the centre of the island.

"Here, let me try," said Flynn. He scrambled past Briar and sat down in front of her. Try as he might, Flynn couldn't get her to alter course either.

They heard a shout, and Elton and Paddy appeared alongside them.

"Iris won't do what I tell her! I don't know where she's taking us!" yelled Flynn.

"Nor will Elton," Paddy replied, and shrugged his shoulders.

The children could do little but enjoy the ride. Eventually, somewhere over the centre of the island, the dragons went into a rapid, spiralling descent. Levelling out, they raced over the treetops of the Colossal Forest until the Mother's Knee Hill came into view. Together, the dragons made for the eastern side, gracefully gliding in to land on the hillside. The children slipped off and stretched their weary bodies, somewhat confused. Elton and Iris, meanwhile, carefully scanned the surrounding countryside.

"What are they doing?" Flynn wondered aloud.

Satisfied, the dragons hopped down into a small hollow in the hillside. There, hidden in the long grass, was a grey and white speckled egg! Together, they put their heads down and gently touched it with their noses, nuzzling it with affection.

Flynn and Paddy looked at each other in disbelief.

"Could this mean there's a baby dragon on the way?" asked Briar.

CHAPTER 29

When the children finally persuaded the dragons to leave their egg and take them home, it was almost dark.

Elton and Iris landed in the soft ferns outside their cottage, and promptly lay down in an exhausted tangle of limbs, tails, and wings.

Equally tired, the children climbed the steps to their home. Before they reached the door, it swung open and their parents tore out, gathering their sons in their arms.

Briar watched as they hugged the boys. Suddenly, she felt very nervous.

"Mum, Dad – this is Briar," said Flynn.

Their mother stepped forward and wrapped Briar in a fierce hug. Briar felt her apprehension melt away. The boys' mother smelled of freshly baked bread and spring flowers – just like her own mother had. Tears of joy came to her eyes. For the first time in years, she felt like she was home.

If you enjoyed reading The Dragon Defenders,
I'd be so grateful if you'd take the time to rate it
or write a review on Amazon.com

Thanks,

Get your FREE copy of The First Defender!

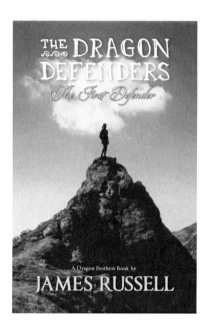

Have you ever wondered what living on a paradise island would be like?

The First Defender – a short novel which you can download for free – includes one of the stories from the diary of Flynn and Paddy's mother. Long before they were born, when she was just a girl – and the only child on The Island – she had some pretty thrilling adventures of her own.
You might even call her the original 'Dragon Defender'.

To get your free copy, visit
dl.bookfunnel.com/i12zk78xaa

About the author

Once, when James Russell was a child, he read a book so exciting it made his heart thump in his chest. Now his aim in life is to write books that will do just that for other children. He hopes that this is one of them.

James lives in Auckland, New Zealand with his wife and two young sons, who love adventure in all its forms.

Also by James Russell

Read all the **Dragon Defenders** books!

 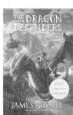 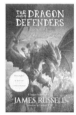 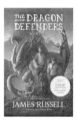 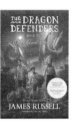

Check out James's new series, **Children of the Rush**

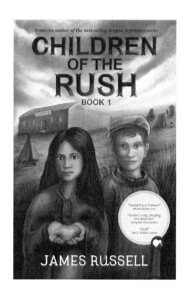

"So thrilling!"
Read New Zealand

"Captivating and fast-paced!"
NZ Booklovers

"Couldn't put it down!"
WhatBookNext.com

"Terrific! Gritty, thrilling, and beautiful!"
Weng Wai Chan, award-winning author

Available on the Amazon store or at
www.dragonbrothersbooks.com